BY SARWAT CHADDA

City of the Plague God

39 Clues: Mission Atomic

Ash Mistry and the World of Darkness

Ash Mistry and the City of Death

The Savage Fortress

Dark Goddess

Devil's Kiss

Minecraft: Castle Redstone

MINECRAFT™
CASTLE
REDSTONE

MINECRAFT™
CASTLE
REDSTONE

SARWAT CHADDA

DEL
REY

NEW YORK

Copyright © 2022 by Mojang AB. All rights reserved.
Minecraft, the MINECRAFT logo, and the MOJANG STUDIOS
logo are trademarks of the Microsoft group of companies.

Published in the United States by Del Rey,
an imprint of Random House, a division of
Penguin Random House LLC, New York.

DEL REY and the CIRCLE colophon are
registered trademarks of Penguin Random House LLC.

Published in the United Kingdom by Century,
an imprint of Random House UK, London.

LIBRARY OF CONGRESS CATALOGING-IN-PUBLICATION DATA
Names: Chadda, Sarwat, author.
Title: Castle Redstone / Sarwat Chadda.
Description: New York: Del Rey, [2022] |
Series: Minecraft | Audience: Ages 10 and up.
Identifiers: LCCN 2022039170 |
ISBN 9780593498538 (hardcover) | ISBN 9780593498545 (ebook) |
ISBN 9780593500972 (international edition)
Subjects: CYAC: Minecraft (Game)—Fiction. |
Adventure and adventurers—Fiction. |
LCGFT: Action and adventure fiction. | Novels.
Classification: LCC PZ7.C343 Cas 2022 | DDC [Fic]—dc23
LC record available at https://lccn.loc.gov/2022039170

Endpaper art: M. S. Corley

Printed in the United States of America on acid-free paper

randomhousebooks.com

2 4 6 8 9 7 5 3

Book design by Elizabeth A. D. Eno

To the gamers, old school and new

MINECRAFT™
CASTLE
REDSTONE

CHAPTER 1

"OW! THAT HURTS!"

"Sorry, sire. I'll be more careful. It's just these arrows are a little tricky to get out. Just lie still for a minute longer. Just one more."

Pal took firm hold of the last arrow. How had they gotten so many right on target? Three straight into Sir Rajah's backside? Good thing there was a lot of padding there or else he could have been badly hurt. He gave it a gentle twist . . . "You're being very brave."

"Of course I am! Brave is my middle name! It'll take a lot more than a . . . ow!"

Pal held the final arrow up. "There! All done!"

He tossed it onto the fire and rummaged around in his backpack. "We're running low on food. We need to head into town and buy some more."

Faith poked the flames to get more life out of them. "With what? We haven't gathered any treasure in weeks. All we've been doing is running away, like we did tonight."

"There were more of those skeletons than we could handle!" snapped Sir Rajah as he tried to pull up his pants. "And we did not run away. We carried out a tactical retreat! It's not the same thing at all." He scoffed. "Anyway, you wouldn't understand such military terms."

"I understand that if we'd done what I suggested, hid among the trees, we wouldn't have gotten surrounded," replied Faith, sullenly.

Rajah scoffed. "Hide? Like cowards? That's not the way of heroes. True heroes face their enemies, stout in heart and sword in hand. Where is my sword?"

Pal picked up the diamond blade. "Here you go, sire. Be careful with it. Heartbreaker's looking a bit . . . crooked."

"Nonsense! This is still the greatest weapon in the realm!" Sir Rajah waved it in a big figure eight. "Those skeletons wouldn't stand a chance now. I'd chop them up, reduce them to nothing but piles of bone dust!"

"Of course you would. They just caught us unawares. They basically cheated. No skeleton mob could stand against the great Sir Rajah and the mighty Heartbreaker, sword of heroes!"

"That's right!" declared Sir Rajah, stabbing the air ferociously. "If they came now I'd slaughter them all! I'd—what was that?"

There was a noise coming from outside the cast of the light from the campfire. Pal grabbed his own weapon, a crude and clumsy stone axe, and peered deeper into the darkness. Something was out there. They'd all heard the crack of a footstep on a brittle twig. The others stood, Sir Rajah moaning as he pulled his pants up over his injured buttocks. Faith stood beside him with her arrow nocked.

Pal looked at his two companions. How had they ended up

like this? They'd left the manor house with such ambitions. They were going to be heroes! They were set on defeating monsters, rescuing the needy, and gathering a towering treasure hoard. But it had degenerated quickly into nights sleeping in the rain, cold and frosty mornings, and bland kelp for meals. Who knew Sir Rajah would be so squeamish about killing animals for food? What he'd give for a few mutton chops right now.

Maybe they needed to admit they weren't up for it. Not everyone was destined to be a hero. They could pack up and go home. Lord Maharajah would take them back, wouldn't he? Deep down he'd know his son wasn't cut out for this life. He'd as much as admitted it to Pal the day they'd left.

Pal tried to remember what his room back at the manor had looked like. What color had the blankets been on his bed? Red? Brown? Whatever the color, it had been warm and cozy.

You're just homesick. You'll get used to it.

Used to what? All this running and screaming? Sleeping every night with one eye open? Listening to Rajah and Faith arguing? Was it worth it?

But what else are you good for? You're a squire.

That was right. His job was to be there for others. To keep Rajah going when things got tough, on nights like these. Pal glanced over his shoulder. Rajah gripped Heartbreaker tightly and was turning around in circles, eyes wide with fear and sweat glistening on his forehead.

There was definitely something out there.

He wished they were more like the Bravos. Now, that was a real bunch of heroes! He'd seen them a while back, returning from some quest, laden with gems and treasure, boasting of the mobs they'd defeated. They'd been clad in the best armor, their

weapons bright and razor-sharp. The whole realm would be singing their saga soon. Rajah had grumbled, promising he'd bring
back twice as much treasure on their next quest, and that had led
them here, lost in the heart of a gloomy forest infested with skeletons and . . . something else.

Pal took a double-handed hold on his axe, and the bow creaked
as Faith drew the arrow fletching to her cheek.

It was coming closer.

What was it? Not a skeleton, that's for sure. He could recognize their rattling plod by now. Not zombies, either. That had
been an even bigger disaster than the skeletons. They'd been
searching an ancient ruin, hoping for some forgotten treasure,
but had taken too long. They'd only explored half the site before
the sun had set and the darkness had been filled by an eerie groaning. The zombies had come shambling out of the surrounding
ruins, woken by the moonlight. They'd been surrounded and it
would have been the end for all three of them if not for Faith.
She'd found an escape route, climbing up and over the ancient
ruins, jumping the perilous gaps between buildings while the
zombies gathered below. It had been close.

"I see it," said Faith.

"See what?" he asked. "I don't see . . ."

Faith loosed an arrow into the darkness. There was a fierce,
angry hiss and suddenly a massive green horror charged out of the
darkness, hissing loudly as Faith shot a second arrow into it.

"A creeper!" yelled Rajah. "Run!"

But Faith had her third arrow already nocked. "We can beat it,
Rajah! You have to stay and fight!"

What should he do? The creature was practically upon them.
Faith's arrow flew wide as the creeper leapt over a fallen tree
trunk.

"Run!" yelled Rajah.

"Fight!" cried Faith, drawing her last arrow.

Run? Fight? Fight? Run?

He didn't know! Why had they ever left the manor?

The creeper began hissing.

Now, that was bad. Really bad.

"He's right! Run!" he yelled as he grabbed Faith's arm, fouling her aim and sending her final arrow arching into the night sky. It didn't matter; he'd make her more later. She glared at him, but he was already pulling her away frantically.

Rajah was way ahead of them, fleeing deeper into the forest. This was the hero he'd sworn to follow? They'd abandoned all their belongings at the campsite!

The hissing stopped.

Pal glanced back. Maybe it had—

The creeper came apart in the center of their camp, the shock wave obliterating everything, filling the small clearing with a blinding white glare. The power of the explosion tore trees from their roots, threw up a wave of dirt and debris, and lifted them all off their feet. Pal screamed as he lost hold of Faith, turning over and over, everything a blur, and then . . . wham! He hit the ground hard, dirt showered over him, and it all went black.

CHAPTER 2

"HOW'S YOUR HEAD?" ASKED Pal as he joined Faith at the small table.

"Still ringing after that creeper blowing up in front of me." Faith rubbed her face. "And these eyebrows aren't gonna grow back anytime soon."

How they'd made it back, he still didn't know. The first thing he'd been aware of after the explosion was waking up in the small, wobbly bed they'd taken back at the inn. He'd heard Rajah downstairs complaining the mutton chops were cold and Faith arguing, again.

Everything was back to how it normally was. Utterly shambolic.

He'd gotten to work on his table. He'd taken out what materials he had packed and quietly started his labor, ignoring the shouts from below. Working with his hands, that was something he could do. Making things gave him a break from all the drama. For a little while, Pal did something . . . satisfying.

Time to show the others the fruits of his labors.

The inn was busy in the way cheap places made their profit, packing people in with the quantity of their food and drink rather than the quality. Faith sat at a table in the corner, but Rajah was nowhere to be seen. Probably stormed off in a huff over the lack of cushions.

"These might cheer you up a little." He dropped the arrows on the table. "A dozen for your quiver. For next time."

Faith grinned as she picked one up. "Nice work, Pal. Look at that fletching. You're an artist, you know that?"

"They're just a handful of arrows, Faith. Nothing special."

She winced as she pricked her finger on the tip. "Next time we come across a creeper, we'll finish it off well before it gets in range. I bet these arrows can shoot to the horizon."

Why was she making such a big deal over a bunch of arrows? They were just a few sticks, feathers, and chips of flint. Now, if he'd had some real materials, he could have made something special . . .

They'd passed the smithy on the way into town. Glancing into the squat, soot-stained building, Pal had seen the smith working on a sword, one whose blade shone with diamonds. Now, *that* was artistry. The adventurer had handed over a heavy purse of emeralds for the smith's work.

Faith slid over a plate of roast chicken pieces. "They're not bad."

He didn't feel hungry but he munched as he idly scanned the crowd. "Where's Sir Rajah?"

"The market. He said he had to meet someone."

"Who?"

Faith shrugged as she slid the arrows into her quiver. She

raised her drumstick. "Here's to our next escapade! May it bring us glory and gold!"

"You're in a cheery mood."

Faith winked at him. "Our luck's gonna change. I can feel it, Pal. We're just finding our feet. Of course there are gonna be a few setbacks to begin with. You don't become heroes like Lord Maharajah overnight. I reckon he must have had a few failures to begin with. It makes the victories taste all the sweeter, eh?"

"I'll tell you when we've had one."

She nudged him. "Come on, Pal. This is just the beginning. I admit, Rajah's not quite the chip off the old block I'd hoped for, but he's got Heartbreaker. Didn't his father use it to defeat the Ender Dragon?"

"That's how the story goes. But it's a long story and Heartbreaker's not the sword it once was. Have you heard how it rings when Rajah hits something with it? It doesn't sound right. Sounds . . . wrong."

"It's a diamond sword. You can't get better than that."

Couldn't you? He wasn't so sure.

"It needs repairing, that's all I'm saying."

Faith sighed. "You'll need diamonds, then?"

And that was the problem, wasn't it? They didn't have any. They didn't have much at all now. Rajah's armor was falling apart, Heartbreaker was going blunt, and all he could manage was making a pile of arrows. They weren't going to be conquering any great fortresses with such a pathetic collection of arms. He finished off the drumstick and tossed it to a stray cat lurking at the edge of the market square. It grabbed it in its all-but-toothless jaw and scampered off. That's what they were, toothless scavengers fighting for scraps.

"You've got that look again," said Faith. She put her arm over his shoulders. "Things will turn around, you just see."

"When, Faith? Don't you get tired of waiting?"

"You just need to—look. The boss is back and it seems like he's found a friend."

Rajah wove his way through the market crowd. He looked . . . odd. He was smiling, actually grinning, and that wasn't normal. He was hauling another man alongside him. A merchant by the looks of him. Rajah pushed a couple of locals aside and dropped himself and his companion on the bench. Rajah's eyes shone brightly. "I've found our next quest. And this is the big one." He nudged the man beside him. "This is the Mapmaker."

The Mapmaker tipped his hat. "Good evening. What a pleasure, nay, honor it is to meet you all."

"Show them what you have," said Rajah.

The Mapmaker sat up straight, all proud and pompous. "What I am about to show you has been passed down from the ancient times. It is a clue to a fortune that outshines all others. You succeed in this quest, my friends, and you'll be more than heroes, you will be legends."

"Just show us what you've got," said Pal. He sounded like another con man. Somehow they all seemed to gather around Rajah, as if they could smell his naïveté. They'd lost plenty already to one trickster or another.

The Mapmaker seemed to notice Pal's wariness, and he cleared his throat as he reached into his bag. "This is an authentic map, my good friends."

The map was a ragged sheet of yellowed tissue paper. The Mapmaker took great care in unfolding it, but his action was still too sharp and the sheet looked ready to crumble apart. Faith drew a nearby candle closer. "So what have we got? Another treasure map?"

Rajah shook his head. "*The* treasure map."

Pal gazed over it. The ink was long faded, and the language unfamiliar, but he could make out a few details. A river, some mountains, a swamp, and a great city. "A map to where?"

Rajah slowly lowered his finger to the city, drawn in faded red ink. "Castle Redstone."

CHAPTER 3

PAL TAPPED THE WRINKLED paper laid out between them.
"Another one? Come on, sire. The man's clearly another fraudster and this? Just another clever fake."

Rajah glared at him. "I indulge your familiarity because of my
father's fondness toward you, Pal. But I am the leader of this
group, I make the decisions, and don't you forget it."

"Did you tell him who you are?"

"Of course. Why should I not?"

"Then he *knows*, sire. He knows how much this means to you,
to your family. Don't let him swindle you. We need to have more
sense."

The Mapmaker sighed, a little theatrically if truth be told. He
began folding up his map. "If you do not believe in its authenticity, then there are other prospective buyers. I bid you good evening."

Rajah grabbed the man's sleeve as he stood. "Just hold on,
good sir. There is no one here who doubts the map's authenticity.
None of any worth, that is."

"Sire, I'm just trying to protect you. This man is just—"

"Enough! I said enough!" Rajah leaned over the table, his eyes burning. "Who is in charge here? Tell me."

Pal knew he should stand up to him, just once. Rajah was still a boy with just a few wispy hairs on his chin, trying to be a big man in a world that didn't care. Pal had been around, and he knew that people like Rajah just got eaten up, unless someone protected them. Hadn't that been exactly what Lord Maharajah had asked him to do? To look out for his son?

"Well?" asked Rajah.

"You, sire." Pal couldn't help himself. He'd spent too many years being a servant to defy him. He wasn't like Faith.

"And don't you forget it, squire."

What could he do? Pal saw the triumph in the Mapmaker's eyes. The swindler could sit there all plump and happy, knowing that whatever Pal said, whatever Pal tried, would fall on deaf ears. The only thing Rajah could hear now were the words "Castle Redstone."

Pal wished he'd never heard the name. It was becoming a curse.

The Mapmaker straightened out his sleeves as he sat back down. "As you can see, the map is very old, very fragile. It is, I will admit, imperfect. The left corner has been damaged, the details blurred. But this is a map that leads to Castle Redstone, I swear it. The doom of many a great hero. How many parties have ventured off into the wilderness to try to find it? The heart of an ancient, long-forgotten civilization. Masters of a technology we nowadays barely comprehend. The secrets of redstone."

Rajah, captivated, drew his fingers ever so gently over the parchment. "My father spent half his life looking for it. A man who found the End, defeated the Ender Dragon itself, but never came close to Castle Redstone. Look at the script, Pal. It comes from those ancient times."

"If you say so, sire."

Rajah darted him an angry look, but then returned to the map. "It confirms some of the story my father told me. Across the uncharted sea, here is the swamp, there is the pass through Lightning Ridge. Think about it! If we reach the castle, imagine what treasures we'd find!"

But there was more to it than that. Rajah lived in his father's shadow. After all, who hadn't heard of the great Lord Maharajah? What must it be like, being the son of the realm's greatest hero? If there was a chance for him to prove himself, then this was it. Finding Castle Redstone. If this map wasn't, like the five before it, a fake. But maybe Faith was right and their luck was turning. It's just that Pal had given up hoping.

"I want it," said Rajah.

Of course you do. And you're a fool.

The Mapmaker smiled indulgently. "Nothing would give me greater pleasure than giving it to the son of the esteemed hero of the realm. But this was not easily acquired. You would not believe the expense. Shocking, really."

"Just get to the price," said Pal.

The Mapmaker leaned over the table. "I can get whatever there is here, in the market. That is whatever is grown, produced, and manufactured in the Overworld. But there are greater treasures in other realms." He waved his hands airily. "Places only heroes could hope to survive. That's where you will find netherite."

"You want to be paid in netherite?" cried Pal. "Are you serious?"

The Mapmaker shrugged, his hand reaching for the map. "If it's too dangerous . . ."

But Rajah slapped his hand onto the map. "Wait."

What was he doing? Pal leaned over the table. "There's only one place you get netherite, and that's in the Nether, sire. You think life is tough here? That's nothing compared with what lurks in the Nether."

"Those dangers have been exaggerated, Pal."

"Even your father feared going into the Nether."

As soon as he said it, Pal realized his mistake. There was no better way of getting Rajah to agree to do a thing than by telling him his father hadn't. He turned to Faith, but she was gazing at the map, too, the eagerness clear in the way her eyes shone. She wanted grand adventure, and that was exactly what a trip into the Nether would be. If they survived.

Which they wouldn't.

He needed them to see sense. "Look, Mr. Mapmaker, can you give us a moment? Go get yourself a slice of cake."

Pal could see the Mapmaker was starting to get anxious. They both knew that the longer they talked, the more likely they would see sense and turn down the deal. The Mapmaker collected the map reluctantly, stood up, and bowed. "I shall leave you to your discussion, but I have other buyers eager for my wares."

Pal waited till he was deep in the market crowd. "It's too dangerous. We barely survived our trip into the forest. We've had our backsides kicked by a bunch of rattlebones. What makes you think we would fare any better in the Nether?"

"How much worse can it be?" asked Faith.

"Oh, believe me, much, much worse." Where to begin? He knew all the tales; so did Rajah. "It's the dark realm separate from ours, and ruled by monsters. If the blazes don't get you, the piglins will."

Faith laughed. "Piglins? They sound cute."

"They are anything but cute. The whole place is flooded by lava. We're not ready to go to the Nether."

Rajah banged his fist on the table. "When will we be ready? When we're clad in diamond armor? When we've got buckets of potions? Are draped in enchanted items? All that comes after, Pal. After we've won great victories, after we've conquered mighty bastions and covered ourselves in glory! The map's authentic, I've seen enough fakes now to recognize the real thing. This is our chance, Pal. Our chance to make names for ourselves, instead of living under the shadow of my father's."

"You don't have to follow in his footsteps, sire. Be your own man. You don't need to chase after this hero stuff. Not everyone's cut out for it."

Rajah's gaze darkened. "What are you trying to say? That I'm not cut out to be a hero?"

"Er . . . your talents may lie elsewhere, that's all I'm saying. We just, er, need to find out what they are."

"Listen to your squire, Rajah. He's talking sense."

Who said that? Pal spun on his stool and saw there was a group gathered around the table beside them.

Oh no.

The Bravos. The realm's toughest, most successful band of heroes. Each one clad in the best armor, polished so brightly they all seemed to sparkle. Their weapons rested on the table, or hung from their belts, and each one was the work of a master craftsman. Their leader, Sir Tyrus, raised a mutton chop. "Stick to roughing up sheep, though I hear you run from them, too. What is it? Their bleating a bit too terrifying?"

"I'm allergic to wool!" snapped Rajah.

Pal sighed. "I really wish you hadn't said that."

The Bravos sat there, stunned into silence. Then they erupted into laughter and bleating. One got up and began prancing around, pretending to be a sheep. Another began running around the table, terrified. It didn't take two guesses to realize who he was imitating.

"Come on, let's go. I've found a place for us to sleep. The landlord's set up some beds in the barn, and the horses seem friendly enough."

"I'm not sleeping in a barn!" snapped Rajah.

"It's all we can afford, sire. Please, let's go."

"Baa! Baa! Baaaa!" cried the Bravos. "Look! They're running away already! Baaaa!"

Pal took hold of Rajah's arm. "Come on, sire."

He resisted, just for a moment, to look back at the Bravos. What did Rajah see? He stiffened, and Pal knew it was jealousy. What else could it be? The Bravos were everything they weren't. Pride and common sense warred behind Rajah's dark eyes. There was that awful thought, always uppermost in Rajah's mind and the one that had led him, led them, into trouble over and over again.

What would Father do?

Rajah's hand fell upon the hilt of Heartbreaker.

The Bravos fell silent. A stool leg scraped upon the cobblestones and Sir Tyrus put his own palm upon the haft of his keen-edged axe. The weapon was sharp, notched from a hundred battles, and could decapitate three zombies with a single swipe. It was old, hard iron, nothing like Heartbreaker, but it had served Sir Tyrus a lifetime. It didn't have a name, but it was a weapon to be afraid of.

Rajah's hand slipped from his sword hilt. "Let's go find that . . . barn. I'm tired."

Phew. He'd seen sense, just in time. This wasn't running away, this was a tactical retreat. "Come on, Faith."

She didn't move. She sat there, glowering at the Bravos. "They're nothing but bullies. We should teach them a lesson."

"Another time, okay? Rajah's not fully healed."

Reluctantly, very reluctantly, she stood up. "Okay, Pal. Another time."

The barn wasn't far. They'd rest up and make new, sensible plans for tomorrow. None of this Nether nonsense. Try to lower their ambitions. Start small and work their way up.

"Baaaa."

Rajah stopped dead.

Pal tugged him along, but he wasn't budging.

"Baaaa. Baaaa."

Why oh why did this have to happen to him tonight? All he wanted was something to eat, a safe warm place to sleep, and maybe something warm for breakfast. Was that too much to ask?

"Baaaa."

Apparently it was.

Rajah turned around. "What did you say?"

Sir Tyrus stood up. "You heard. Now shuffle along, boy. This area is for the grown-ups."

"I am no child. My name is Rajah and I am the son of Lord—"

"Who cares? If your sword arm was as active as your mouth then perhaps you'd amount to something but, and I speak for everyone here, no one is interested in that windbag of a father of yours. All those adventures he had?" Sir Tyrus snapped his fingers. "Just tales he paid the bards to spread. I wouldn't be surprised if has plenty of arrow wounds in his backside, too, from all the running away he must have done. That's what you've inherited, boy. His cowardice."

That was a big mistake. Sir Tyrus could have gotten away with throwing muck at Rajah, but not with throwing it at his father.

Rajah drew Heartbreaker from his sheath. "You take that back."

"And if I don't?"

"We settle it right here, right now, and find out who the real coward is."

Sir Tyrus grinned as reached for his axe. "I'd like nothing better."

CHAPTER 4

THEY'D CLEARED THE MARKETPLACE pretty quickly. The locals packed themselves among the stalls that lined the perimeter, leaving a large, empty space. An arena. The Bravos gathered in one corner, clustered around their leader. Sir Tyrus was taking big swings with his axe and even from here, above the hubbub and chatter, Pal heard it whistling through the air.

Meanwhile here they were, in the opposite corner, pale and just a little bit terrified.

Rajah swallowed hard, then began his stretches. "Just because he's bigger, stronger, faster, and more experienced than me doesn't mean he's going to win."

"We need to use his strengths against him," said Faith.

They both turned to her.

"How?" said Rajah, his voice quivering with desperate hope.

"I don't know, it's just a thing people say, when the hero faces some undefeatable monstrosity, isn't it? He's got to have a weakness. Pal, don't make it too obvious, but check out his knees."

"His what?"

"His knees. Maybe they're fragile. A weak spot. After all, they need to support a whole load of muscle."

Pal looked over, then shook his head. "His legs are like tree trunks."

"Victory is inevitable," declared Rajah as he drew Heartbreaker. "My father's sword will not fail me in my hour of need."

Not for the first time Pal wished he'd never set eyes on that weapon. Heartbreaker. Who gives names to weapons? Why? Tyrus's axe had no name and didn't seem any lesser for it. The trouble with putting names on weapons was you expected them to do all the hard work for you, conveniently forgetting it was the person behind them that made them what they were. In this case, legends.

But Heartbreaker's legend had been made a long time ago. Pal winced as Rajah took a couple of big swipes. Was it his imagination or was the blade a little . . . wobbly?

"We could always apologize," he said.

"For what? He insulted my father!" snapped Rajah. "The man who practically raised you!"

Raised me as a servant. I never got to sit at the table, did I? Raised me to do his bidding, and now yours.

Why didn't he just leave? Why drag himself along from one peril to another, wading through the mud and thickets on some fresh, foolish quest? What difference did it make to him if Rajah succeeded or failed? If they sang of Rajah's exploits around the campfires and in the manor houses, was his name ever mentioned? Of course not. You couldn't share glory without diminishing it. And Rajah needed to hang on to every scrap of glory he could, paltry nuggets of copper against the great golden ingots of

his father's. That was it, wasn't it? Pal had nothing to measure up
to, so he never bothered. He expected nothing of himself, so he
didn't try. Why even attempt to climb? The height will make you
dizzy. You're not used to being anything except down on the bottom rung, holding the ladder steady for others.

That's all you're good for.

Maybe. Maybe.

What could he do about it? Leave tomorrow. Just as the sun
came up. Make a life of his own. But right now he was needed.
Pal looked over Rajah's armor. The straps of the chest plate
needed new stitches, but they'd hold for now. And the helmet?
That dent should have been knocked back out ages ago but they
never seemed to get the chance. Too late now. All he needed was
the right tools and some better materials, then he could have
crafted Rajah a real suit of armor . . .

Someone approached them through the eager crowd. "Well?
Are you ready?"

It was . . . what was her name? Lady Payne? Sir Tyrus's right-
hand woman. She gestured over her shoulder to her waiting companions. "The boss wants to finish his dinner and it's getting cold."

Rajah shoved the helmet on. "What, er, what are the rules
again?"

"Rules?" Payne frowned, then laughed. "This is going to be so
much fun."

Pal watched her walk back, heart sinking. This wasn't about
winning anymore, this was about surviving. He didn't want Rajah
getting hurt too badly. But maybe this could be a good thing. Finally make it clear that this wasn't the life for them, any of them.
They could then head home, a little battered but a lot wiser.

It was a treacherous thought, but Pal couldn't help it being there. He wanted the best for Rajah, he really did. Maybe this was for the best. He handed over the shield. "Keep this in front of you. Let him tire himself out smashing into it. Then look for an opening, any opening. Go for the knees if you have to. Lure him into a false sense of superiority."

"False?" asked Rajah.

Faith did the last few adjustments. "Just remember the lessons your father taught you."

Rajah looked pale under his helmet. "All of them? There were so many and it all got a little confusing at times. I could never remember my left from my right. And Father tended to shout a lot. Made it hard to concentrate."

The crowd cheered. Sir Tyrus waited in the center of the market square, the torchlight illuminating his brightly polished armor. He looked . . . magnificent. Every inch the hero. Rajah? A . . . work in progress?

Rajah gulped loudly. "This is it, then."

"Keep your shield up and look for an opening," said Pal.

"You've got this," said Faith. "You're Sir Rajah and don't you forget it." She started pumping her fist in the air. "Rajah! Rajah! Rajah!"

And guess what? Some of the crowd, not much of it, but some, took up her chant. Maybe that could make all the difference. Rajah did seem to be standing a little taller . . .

But even then he came up only to Sir Tyrus's chest. The pair faced each other and the difference between them was painful. Maybe attacking the knees was a sensible strategy: Rajah could hardly reach any higher.

"Keep your shield up," muttered Pal.

"Remember who you are," said Faith.

Sir Tyrus didn't bother with a shield. He took up his axe with both hands. The haft was as thick as a tree bough and yet his fingers circled it easily. He held it aloft and the crowd *roared*.

Faith nudged Pal as she started chanting. "Rajah! Rajah! Rajah!"

Pal took up the call, trying to raise the crowd. But after a few halfhearted cheers, it fell silent. He looked over at the duelists. It was on.

CHAPTER 5

AND JUST LIKE THAT, it was over.

It took a moment for Pal, for everyone, to realize. To realize that Rajah stood there in a sprinkle of diamond dust, all that was left of Heartbreaker.

Legendary Heartbreaker. The sword that Lord Maharajah had wielded on all his great quests. The sword that had slain the Ender Dragon.

"What . . . what happened?" asked Faith. "I must have blinked."

Even Sir Tyrus looked . . . bewildered? He wasn't the only one. Pal decided to play it over again in his head. It didn't take long.

"What was that squeak?" said Faith. "I thought someone had trodden on a mouse."

"That was Rajah's battle cry. I might have buckled the helmet on a bit too tight."

"It's . . . over?"

"Yeah. Very." That was that, then. "Come on. Rajah needs us."

He wanted to get to him before things turned really bad. Before people started—

"Look at the brave Sir Rajah! What's wrong, hero? Someone broken your toy? Boo hoo!"

"Hero? Clown more like!"

—too late.

The laughter erupted. It didn't build, it burst from the crowd as it finally clicked in for them that the duel was over. That what they'd seen was all there was to see. What they'd lost in nail-biting drama, in the heart-stopped tension and the breathless dance of blades, had been replaced by sheer buffoonery.

Pal ran up to Rajah, who was just standing there, gazing at his empty hand. There was a faint coating of diamond dust on his glove.

"Are you hurt, sire?"

"I didn't even touch him!" declared Sir Tyrus. "He just swung his sword and I . . . I just raised my axe to block and . . . well. It just broke."

Broke? Broke would have meant there was something for him to gather up and stick back together again. Heartbreaker had shattered into diamond dust. There was no gathering it except with a dustpan.

Pal faced up to the knight. "Satisfied?"

"Not really." Sir Tyrus shrugged. "Those chops will be cold by now."

Rajah wasn't speaking. He wasn't even blinking. Faith joined up with them; standing either side of him, together she and Pal led him through the hysterical crowd. Rajah seemed oblivious to it all, and maybe that was a good thing, but everywhere Pal looked he saw mockery, ridicule, contempt. The crowd jeered and laughed. They imitated Rajah's stunned shock, played out the brief, painfully brief, fight. Swing, smash. All over. They wanted to make it last, so they followed them down the street, calling after

Rajah to try again. They wanted to challenge him, too, with their hoes, bread loaves, anything close at hand. But slowly they gave up and returned to the celebration in the market square with the Bravos. Why hang out with losers when there were real heroes in town?

Where was that barn? They were lost in the alleyways now, but at least Rajah was talking. Mumbling to himself. Then he stopped dead and covered his face with his hands and started sobbing. "It's all over."

Now what should he do? Pal patted him on the back. "There, there. It'll be fine."

"Fine? Fine?" From misery to raw, volcanic anger in an eye-blink. Rajah thrust his face mere inches from Pal's. "In case you weren't paying any attention I've just lost Heartbreaker! My father's sword!"

"Yes, well . . . I did say it looked a little wobbly."

"And whose fault is that? Yours, Pal! Yours! You were meant to look after it! Make sure it stayed sharp and didn't shatter the moment I swung it!"

"I didn't have the materials—"

"Excuses! That's all I get from you. What else should I have expected? You have no ambitions, no dreams."

Faith stepped between them. "It's no one's fault, Rajah. We're all trying our best."

"That's your best?" snapped Rajah. "Nothing's gone right since you joined up! And why do you call me Rajah? I'm a noble, you should show me more respect!"

Faith shot Pal a glance, then turned back to Rajah. "You're just upset."

"Of course I am! With both of you. What's the point? You

don't understand," said Rajah, miserably. "You're happy just the way you are."

Happy? Did Rajah know anything about him? How could he be happy trailing along behind him?

He should tell him what he thought, right now. But somehow the words died before they crossed the fateful barrier of his teeth, before they could do real harm. They were in this together, for now.

Why had he made that promise to Lord Maharajah? Did he owe the family that much? And what was a promise anyway? Could breaking it hurt any more than losing Heartbreaker? Would Rajah even notice, even care? Did Rajah care about anything but himself?

Just look at him. He's given up, just like that.

Rajah slumped against a wall, not caring he was sitting amid refuse and market dregs. Why was it always Pal's job to lift him up?

"That's it then," said Pal. "We tried but it didn't work out."

Faith looked at him, bemused. "What do you mean?"

Pal gestured to the main road running through the village. "If we start off early we could be back at the manor by the end of the week. Quicker, if the weather's good."

Now she looked shocked. "You're giving up? Just like that?"

Why couldn't she see what was plain right in front of her? "We're not cut out for this life, Faith. Rajah's not like his father. There's no point trying anymore."

"So he got beaten. So what? That's life. You and I know it. But you can't just roll over, let the bullies win. You gotta defy them."

"Defiant in defeat? That's not how things are, Faith."

"Wrong." She crossed her arms. "That's exactly how things are."

He had to decide. There was so much he could do, out there and unencumbered by Rajah. All it meant was breaking a simple promise. Then living with it.

"I'm just going for a walk," he said.

Faith frowned. "Where?"

"Just for a walk. Wait here for a while."

Pal turned away before she could ask any more questions, ones he couldn't answer. He left the alleyway and it was as though he was breaking free of the gloom, as though some fresh breeze had just blown the fog away. This was what it could be like, if he was free.

And why not? *Just keep walking. Don't look back. That's your old life and it was miserable, wasn't it?*

Rajah was a failure, time to acknowledge that. *Be honest, and save yourself a lifetime.* He was never going to measure up to his father and each setback, tonight only the latest of many, would drag not just him but everyone else around him down lower and lower. Eventually there'd be nothing left. People like that were just a millstone around your neck; best cut them free to sink in the quagmire alone. It was foolish to hope tomorrow would be any better.

Whichever way you looked at it, leaving was the best thing for all of them. Maybe without Heartbreaker, Rajah would finally see sense and go home. Live a quiet life and somehow get used to his father's disappointment. Not everyone was cut out to be a hero.

Torchlight flickered from the windows of the buildings that lined the street. They weren't anything special, these constructions, plain blocks built without imagination, just copies of everyone else. What was the name of this town? He had no idea. Did it matter? There were thousands just like it scattered over the realm. Few places had names worth remembering.

Not like Castle Redstone.

It was out there, somewhere. The heart of a civilization that was long gone, but a place of wonder and of marvels. Lord Maharajah's manor had contained a few redstone circuits, nothing special, but Pal remembered marveling at how the pistons worked, how the levers activated doors, and even the simple railway that had been built to travel around the grounds. He and Rajah would spend all day going around and around, rocking back and forth in the carts, the wheels going clickety-clack. Imagine an entire city like that. Everything working by a simple press of a button or tug on a lever. Buildings that moved, that could alter their shapes, a city that transformed itself every morning into something new.

He didn't even know he was doing it until he reached the outskirts of the market square. The crowd had gone, the Bravos were nowhere to be seen, but there, by one of the food stalls, sat the Mapmaker.

Pal crossed the square and sat down opposite him before he knew it. "How do I know that map's for real?"

"So the lord sends his servant to haggle, is that it? To drive the price down a bit?" The Mapmaker straightened his cuffs. "The price is what it is."

"Netherite? For a faded piece of parchment? Even if the map's real, you need to get to the Nether. That's no mere stroll down the lane."

"Leave that to me," said the Mapmaker.

Pal didn't like the sound of that, but then he didn't like the sound of any of this . . . adventure.

Why was he doing this? This guy was another fraudster, he was sure of it. Pal should just turn around and go back . . . to what?

A dejected Rajah? An impatient Faith? They needed a purpose, and this was all that was on offer.

And what if, *what if*, the map was authentic?

"We'll need gear. A journey to the Nether's dangerous even for the most tooled-up party."

"Leave that to me," said the Mapmaker.

Was he being as foolish as Rajah? He should start small and build up toward this. Not hurl himself headfirst into the perils of the dark realm at the first opportunity. But if that map was real . . .

Pal thrust out his hand. "A deal."

The Mapmaker didn't take it. "What about the others? Will you be able to persuade them to join you?"

For a chance to find Castle Redstone? "Leave that to me."

The Mapmaker smiled, and *then* they shook hands.

"What took you so long? It's past midnight!" Faith gestured behind her at Rajah, curled up and asleep. "He actually cried himself to sleep. Now what are we going to do? You said you'd found a barn—"

"Forget about the barn. Just let him sleep where he is. You'll need to get some rest yourself. Tomorrow's a big day."

Faith narrowed her gaze. "You're up to something. What?"

He and the Mapmaker had talked after the deal had been struck. Talked about what to expect, what needed doing, and exactly where to go to get the netherite. Pal had the suspicion that they weren't the first party the Mapmaker had sent down there. What had happened to the others? He hadn't asked. Best not to know. He had enough things to worry about.

"Why do you tag along, Faith? You don't owe Rajah anything," asked Pal. "You're too smart to be taken in by the stories about his father. Even if half of them are true, they've grown in the telling.

No one's *that* good. You know he didn't beat that Ender Dragon by himself. It's just that his companions got left out of the tale once and never got back in."

"Why do you stay?" she asked.

"I'm the squire. What's a knight without a squire? Or a squire without a knight?"

"Really? Is that why you took so long to come back?"

She wasn't a fool. But then why was she so keen on following one? "What do you want, Faith?"

"Something different, that's all."

That was as good an answer as any. He'd been stuck with years of the same, and it hadn't done him any good. "Something different would be fine by me, too."

"What about the boss?" Faith looked over her shoulder at the curled-up Rajah. He had his thumb in his mouth. It was hard to believe he was the son of the realm's greatest hero.

"He needs something different more than any of us. No way is he going to survive for long going about business the way he has been."

"So what are we going to do?"

What indeed? The odds were stacked against them. The Nether. That was a fool's errand. Just so happened here they were, a bunch of fools. They'd been getting by on Rajah's famous family name and a few swings of Heartbreaker when it mattered. Those days were over, and they'd been lean days anyway.

"We're going to make Rajah a hero. Even if it kills him."

CHAPTER 6

"YOU WANT ME TO go through that?" Rajah backed away from them. "No way!"

"We'll be there with you. It's perfectly safe," said Pal. Then he turned to the Mapmaker. "It's perfectly safe, right?"

The Mapmaker smiled cheerily. "I'm sure you'll be mostly fine."

They'd met him outside the town early in the morning. They'd passed abandoned buildings and a few empty farms until they'd come to this place, a clearing upon a hilltop. And here stood the portal.

He'd heard about portals, of course. Heard from adventurers who'd traveled through them. Lord Maharajah had jumped through one in order to conquer his first fortress, but the way he'd described the experience, it had felt like it was a mere construction.

Not this portal. It felt alive. It felt as if it had a mind, a will. A hunger. The obsidian ate the light, creating something more than darkness, creating a void that, if you stared into it, seemed to grow and grow, seemed to want to swallow you whole. Maybe Rajah had a point.

Faith didn't look any more confident than he did. She walked around it several times, clockwise and counterclockwise. "How does it work exactly?"

"No one really knows for sure," said the Mapmaker, more casually than Pal would have liked. But then it wasn't him going through it, was it?

"And you expect us to just jump right in?" asked Faith.

"Remind me what your name is again." The Mapmaker walked over to a long wooden table under the shadow of a half-built roof. "I've gathered some equipment you may find handy."

"Any enchanted items? Or potions?" said Rajah as he hurried over. "Dibs on the magic swords."

They should be so lucky. This gear was a jumbled assortment of weapons and armor, a few stacks of ladders. Pal picked up a helmet. The front had melted. "And what happened to the previous owner?"

The Mapmaker cleared his throat as he hefted an iron sword. "How about this?"

"It's bent. What's it for? Stabbing around corners?"

Rajah was looking more and more aghast. "Whenever Father went on a quest he had a whole armory of enchanted gear! Arrows that burst into flames! Potions that doubled his strength! Even a pair of wings. I tried them once, to fly around the manor. Or at least tried to. I ended up in the pond."

Faith inspected a crossbow. "Why does that not surprise me?"

Pal shot her a glance but Faith just winked. She was actually enjoying this. Pal felt sick. Talking about going into the Nether had seemed easier last night, when they'd been desperate and angry, but now the sun was up and it seemed perfectly idiotic to throw themselves from this world into a world of darkness and terror. There had to be better, safer options, right? How did other people get by? Collect a few chickens and sheep, and start a farm. Maybe that was the life he should be leading. Nothing wrong with that.

But as he gazed at the portal, the shimmering purple void at the heart of it, he knew he was no farmer. And it had nothing to do with Rajah being allergic to wool. "Try this, sire."

He'd built it last night. It wasn't much, but it was all they had.

"A stone axe?" said Rajah. "But I'm a knight, not some rampaging illager vindicator! Knights have shiny swords! Everyone knows that!"

"We need to start somewhere, sire. This will do the job. Trust me."

Rajah opened his mouth to complain, then took a swing with it. "Until I find something better, I suppose this will have to do."

And that was about as much of a compliment as he could hope for. But that axe wouldn't snap with the first blow, unlike the bent sword the Mapmaker was offering.

They stood before the glowing opening. Was it his imagination or did he feel a fiery gust?

The Nether. A realm of fire and darkness. The abode of the sinister ghasts, of blazes and other terrors. But it was also a place where fortunes could be made. Vast fortunes.

"Oh, I should have mentioned this earlier, but you may have some competition at the bastion you're headed for," said the Mapmaker.

"Popular place, is it?" asked Pal.

"It has a great store of netherite. Just waiting to be picked up.

The trouble is, word gets around and another band of heroes is equally keen to claim such a fortune."

Pal had a bad feeling about this "other band of heroes." "Anyone we know?"

The Mapmaker adjusted his cuffs. Pal didn't like the way he did it, like he was shaking off something unpleasant. "The Bravos have built themselves a portal and already gone through. An enterprising bunch, whatever else you may think of them."

Rajah turned to face him. "If they are so wonderful why didn't you ask them to go on this mission instead of us?"

"He did, they said no," replied Faith, her eyes wide as she gazed at the shimmering portal. "Isn't that right?"

The Mapmaker didn't answer, but his blushing face confirmed it.

"Maybe we should hold hands?" suggested Rajah. "Only if you're scared. Which I am not."

Why not? Maybe that might prevent them from ending up at three completely different locations. Pal tried not to imagine arriving over a river of lava. Or a horde of ravenous piglins. Or a haunting of Endermen. Or a—

Stop it. You can do this.

The wind was howling through now, as hot as if straight from a furnace. Rajah's fingers squeezed his so tightly they started to go numb.

The Mapmaker was shouting his final instructions. "One more thing! An old rival of mine built a great iron door to guard the entrance to the treasure room. You'll need to find a way to open it. Beyond that lie riches beyond imagining!"

Pal faced the portal, willing his legs to jump. "What's this about a rival?"

"He's long gone, but his iron door remains," said the Mapmaker. "Find the bastion! Get through the door to the treasure room! That's where the netherite's kept!"

"Another other tips?" yelled Faith.

"Yes! Whatever you do, make sure you don't—"

Then the world Pal knew wobbled and disappeared.

CHAPTER 7

FAITH WAS SCREAMING. RAJAH was screaming. Pal was screaming. They hurtled through the roaring, howling darkness. Faith imagined claws trying to grasp her, nails clutching at her hair, at her clothes, trying to hold her, trap her in the nowhere space between the Overworld and the Nether. Who or what else was trapped in this terrible space between realms? She didn't want to know, but for a dreadful, heart-chilling moment she imagined herself stuck here and howling in despair for eternity. She hung on to Rajah, locking her fingers, feeling that at least he was real when everything else was a pandemonium of eerie sounds and skin-crawling sensations. They fell and fell, twisted over and over, at one moment blasted by an unbearable heat and then the next by a blood-freezing chill. How many other realms were there? Was this emptiness the gap between more than just the world she knew and the Nether? Could there be more, countless more, just beyond this darkness? What hands and minds had created them?

It was too much. She couldn't understand it. She was just a simple farm girl, trying to make something of herself. Leave the world-building to the vaster, incomprehensible minds.

Then . . .

She broke through a barrier of swirling violet and left the desperate, imprisoned spirits behind. Faith blinked, shaking her head until her eyes came back into focus. Rajah relaxed his grip.

"I don't believe it," he said. "We did it."

Faith stared at the rivers of lava flowing across their path. The heat turned the air into a shimmering wall beyond which she could see a vast, eerie landscape of dark purple, deep blues, and greens. It was the realm, inverted.

"We made it," she whispered to herself.

Perhaps there was more to Rajah and Pal. She'd joined them, not that long ago, hoping to go on great adventures, travel far beyond the drear town she'd been raised in. She'd seen adventurers come and go, trade with her people, spend a night or two feasting, healing, recounting tales of the mobs they'd defeated, and dazzling the locals with the treasures they'd found. Gems, enchanted weapons, gold and diamonds and purses filled with emeralds. She'd then gone back to her farm with the sheep and chickens, feeding them but dreaming of something . . . more.

To cross over the horizon, to go beyond the fields and hills of her home. To walk along the road and look not back, but forward. No one understood her. Why was she unhappy? She had a roof over her head, never went hungry, and had friends aplenty. What more could she want? The world beyond was dangerous. Hadn't she been listening to the stories? Of the monsters that lurked out in the wilderness? Of zombies and skeletons, of Endermen and creepers? She met only the adventurers who survived. What about those others who never made it back? Blown up by the roaming creepers or slaughtered by illagers? Is that how she wanted her life to end?

Live a small, safe life. Don't take risks. Do what you're told and stick to what you know. There's nothing wrong with being unexceptional. A face in the crowd.

Her family meant well; they wanted the best for her. There was nothing wrong with that. But what sort of life would it have been if she'd never even *looked* at what else was out there?

So one night after having fed the chickens, having gathered the sheep and finished watering the plants, she'd packed up her rucksack, gathered her walking stick, laced up her boots, and left. She'd looked back once, just at the crest of the hill that marked the boundary of her town. The moon had shone on the roofs. All the houses had looked the exact same; she wasn't even sure which was her own home. The same, and nothing ever changed. The wind seemed to summon her, wanting to gently nudge her along, and away.

Her first night on the road, and almost her last . . .

Who'd thought it could get so dark? And who'd thought she'd get lost so quickly? The road had diminished to a lane, then a path, and then she'd found herself in a forest with no path at all. The dense canopy hid the pale light from the glowstones embedded in the ceiling and smothered the eerie luminescence off the shroomlights clinging to the trunks of the giant fungi. The surrounding shadows seemed to grow even as she stared at them, trying to swallow her. They seemed to be swallowing everything else.

There's nothing to be scared of. You've been here before, searching for mushrooms.

But it all looked so different in the dark. The noises were more ominous. The wind moaned through the trees, rustling the leaves like so many bones. The creaking boughs sent shivers up her back.

She'd brought her bow. The weapon had been left behind by another adventurer and she'd spent days, weeks, struggling to shoot with it. The skin had torn off her fingers, her arms and shoulders had ached horribly, and the arrows had barely flown. But then one had hit the old target block she'd found. That first hit, that one success had been all she needed.

But what use was her bow when she couldn't even see? Still, Faith nocked an arrow. Running her fingers along the neat fletching gave her the belief she wasn't just some hopeless victim, but someone capable of changing things.

And there was no turning back. Her old life was gone forever. That much she knew right down deep in her bones.

The rustling came from all around her. But there was another sound—footsteps barely heard over the whisper of wind through the fungus trees.

This wasn't a story anymore. This wasn't her sitting around the hearth, all warm and cozy and listening to some grand tale. This was real, and this was happening right now.

A shape moved through the pillars of darkness ahead of her. Faith drew on her bowstring, wincing as the bow creaked under the strain. The thing turned its head and hissed all the louder.

Faith's fingers froze on the bowstring even as the creeper crept closer. It wasn't far; she couldn't miss. But her heart thundered in her chest and her arms trembled as she tried to aim. Ever closer the mob came. She shot, too hastily.

The first arrow went wide, disappearing forever into the undergrowth. The creeper stalked closer.

The second arrow nocked, Faith forced herself to be still. She took a deep breath even as it stalked between the trees and leapt over the mossy boulders. Faith waited and then, in a single, oft-practiced move, drew the arrow to her chin and loosed it as the thing swung around a broad tree trunk. That moment it stopped to change direction, and that moment she had her target.

The second arrow stunned it, making it falter. The third struck it dead-center, knocking it back, momentarily. But it still continued coming, its whole body trembling as it began hissing again.

The fourth arrow was what did it.

No explosion this time. It just . . . expired. Faith approached the spot it had just been standing, but nothing of it remained. No trophy, no proof of what she'd done. That didn't matter. She'd done it. She'd defeated her first mob.

She was on her way.

"We'd better be on our way."

"What?" asked Faith.

Pal pointed along the edge of the lava river. "Be on our way?"

She'd destroyed a creeper, but what else lurked in the Nether? Not many adventurers ever made it down here, and even fewer made it back. Hands on her hips, Faith peered along the winding river. Was that a hill in the distance, or the bastion? "Sooner we get there, the sooner we get back."

"If we get back," said Pal.

"We've got this. And do you want the Bravos to have all the fun? All the glory? We're better than them."

"Our present, near-destitute situation would imply otherwise. We're not ready for this. We should have waited."

"Some people end up waiting their whole lives, Pal. Then the moment's gone."

"Is this one of those 'seize the day' pep talks? Don't bother. I've heard them all before." He gestured at Rajah, who was up ahead swiping at vines with his axe. "From him. Not recently, though. Rajah's starting to realize that things don't just fall in his lap because he's got a famous dad. The mobs don't seem to care when he shouts 'Do you know who I am?'"

They entered a glade of vine-draped giant cyan-colored fungi. Strange red and brown mushrooms sprouted in among the sprawling roots, and strange dark creatures wandered through the undergrowth.

Rajah raised his axe, but Pal stopped him. "They're Endermen. Best give them a wide berth."

"They're hideous," said Rajah, weapon still aloft.

"Let's not go looking for a fight," said Faith. "I've a feeling we'll have plenty of those ahead of us."

"I could have handled it," said Rajah, sounding as if he was trying to reassure himself.

Faith brushed her hand against a trunk. The bark was burned to charcoal, and still warm. She pulled her bow from her shoulder and nocked an arrow. "Pal . . ."

"What?"

"Something's here," she said. "Rajah! Keep your eyes open!"

But Rajah was busy plucking cobwebs from his hair. "For what?"

Yeah, for what? She smelled the ash in the air. Another huge fungus with its vines crispy and steaming. The leaves had all shriveled with the heat. "Something hot."

Rajah scoffed. "In case you hadn't noticed, there's a river of lava flowing on the other side of the trees."

"Just ready your axe, Rajah."

Something fiery had been hurled through the trees. One tree was now just a black, charcoal stump. A direct hit from . . . what?

Pal gasped, staring straight ahead.

She followed his gaze.

Through the thicket she could make out something approaching from the wastes beyond the boundary of the warped forest. It looked like mist at first, a pale, moonlit glowing patch floating just above the surface of the glade.

"What is it?" Rajah whimpered. He held his stone axe in his trembling hands.

It continued to rise, a bewitching phantom, seemingly made of vapor and malice. Flames flickered in the depths of its gaping mouth.

The leaves around it crackled and smoked as it rose to hover a few feet above the ground. The vapors swayed beneath its pale body.

They couldn't go back, and there was a barrier of flowing lava on her left. If they stayed really quiet, it might not—

"Run!" screamed Rajah. "Run for your lives!"

The roaring fireball vomited out from the creature's maw, flying over Rajah's head and obliterating a nearby tree and hurling Faith backward. The tree burst into flames and the gloomy woods was suddenly lit by ever-shifting orange light and dancing shadows.

Faith staggered unsteadily to her feet and groggily nocked another arrow, but her head was spinning and the arrow flew off into the darkness. She heard the others shouting but the sound of the explosion echoed in her ears. She reached for another arrow . . .

Her quiver was empty.

The explosion had thrown her head over heels and her precious arrows now lay scattered across the ground. She needed to get them back or she was useless. Faith stumbled forward and—

Another explosion showered her with burning vegetation as a second fungus erupted into flame. She untangled herself from the patch of twisting vines she'd landed in. Staying still was only going to get her blasted.

"Run, Faith!" shouted Pal.

"It's a ghast!" yelled Pal. "We can't defeat it!"

"We're not running!" snapped Faith. "Not anymore!"

"Make for the portal!" shouted Rajah. "I didn't want to go to Castle Redstone anyway!"

What were they doing? "Turn around! Fight!"

Rajah tossed the axe as he dashed past. "Be my guest! Come on, Pal!"

"Right behind you, sire!"

The ghast rose above the giant fungus. It had a perfect view over the glade and the stark, desolate Nether Wastes beyond. As soon as they reached the edge of the forest, they'd be exposed. The ghast would incinerate them. But first it needed to deal with her. If only she could get to her arrows!

The fireball shot down toward her. Faith dodged—barely— and the fireball shattered the netherite behind her.

Rajah was already out of the trees. The ghast would be on him in moments.

Faith dropped her bow and snatched up the axe. "Hey! You big cloud of steam! Come on then!"

The ghast opened its mouth all the wider. Fireballs spewed out. Faith ducked beneath one, sidestepped another, but the third, the one that came true and straight, she took a firm grip on the axe haft and swung at, slamming the flat of the stone blade against the fireball and sending it straight back in a shower of burning embers.

The fireball smashed into the ghast and it screamed. It turned black with smoke as the flames briefly flickered across its body, but then it released another barrage of fireballs. One after the other Faith swung, smashing them back the way they'd come. A few flew wild, but one hit, then another, each one erupting as it collided with the floating ghast. It was smoking now, its body aflame, yet its hate was undiminished. It wasn't interested in the two that were fleeing; it had to destroy *her*.

Faith smirked. "Come on then. I'm right here."

The scorn in her voice was all the ghast could take. The fireball, larger than the rest, exploded from its mouth. It swept down through the trees, setting the patch of canopy alight and flooding the dark glade with a blinding wave of heat.

Faith swung with all her might. The impact shuddered through the weapon, through her whole body.

The moment she hit the fireball she knew it was done. The fiery missile flew straight back the way it had come, creating a flare that burned her eyes.

It hit the ghast dead-center and the mob disintegrated into a cloud of thick smoke. Faith watched the wisps dissipate, making sure it was really gone, then sank to her knees, exhausted.

Pal looked down at her. "Faith? Are you hurt?"

That was something, wasn't it? He was concerned. Maybe they were a party after all, each member as valuable as the other. Equals in the face of danger. "I'm just resting a moment."

"It's just Rajah wants his axe back."

"Oh. Of course." So much for being equals.

"It's just you're gripping it rather tightly."

"Oh. Sorry." She turned her head to the axe, locked in her right hand. The blade was scorched where the fireballs had been batted back, but the edge looked keen. She had to consciously force her fingers to open.

Pal picked it up. He glanced back toward Rajah. "That was unbelievable. Best not mention it again, though. You know how Rajah is."

She got back up to collect her arrows, glancing over toward their leader. The son of a legendary hero. He was busy inspecting his fingernails, tapping his foot impatiently. He caught her gaze. "Well? We need to get a move on!"

The guy was a coward. There was no getting away from it. But somehow she couldn't bring herself to say anything. Why? She'd defied family expectations, and wasn't Rajah in the same dilemma? Everyone expected him to be just like his dad. Why? Why did people believe that's how the world worked best? You followed blindly in the footsteps of those who'd marched before you, as if they'd known any better.

We're all just making it up as we go along.

"Look at this, Faith."

Pal was crouched at the spot the ghast had risen from. Thick, noxious vapors still clung to the ground, reluctantly parting as Faith joined him. Pal ran his palm over what looked like gray gravel. "This showered down from the ghast when it was destroyed."

"What is it?"

Pal sniffed it and licked a grain off his finger, wincing. "Some sort of explosive powder. It must be what fueled the ghast's fireballs." He scooped up a handful and poured it carefully into a pouch. "Makes you wonder what you could do with it."

"Isn't it dangerous?"

"I hope so." He looked at her and winked. "Between us, for now."

"I hardly think our boss would be interested."

And right on cue, there he was. Rajah grabbed his axe from Pal and glared at them both. "We need to get a move on right now." And with that he turned and marched off. "The bastion is that way!"

Collecting her bow Faith followed, Pal beside her. They pushed their way through the dank glade and were soon climbing. The lava poured down in immense waterfalls, roaring and hissing as it splashed on the banks. In the distance they spotted roaming mobs, thankfully trapped on the opposite bank. Trees, their leaves deep and bloody crimson, covered the slope, and all around them grew strange plants and fungi of unnatural colors and peculiar odors. More than once she'd felt a presence at her shoulder, would spin, her heart racing, but find nothing there. The wind carried whispers, strange, unintelligible words and warnings, and Faith wondered what happened to those who never made it out of the Nether. "We do know how to get back to our portal, don't we?"

Rajah stopped, glancing at her with a condescending curl of his lip as he reached into his pocket and pulled out a small disk-shaped object. "Of course. You just follow the compass here. It has never led me . . . oh. That can't be right."

It wasn't. They tested the compass by turning in all four cardinal directions, but the needle just spun wildly.

Faith gazed down from their lofty plateau. Under the nether-rack dome, ominously the color of dried blood, the landscape was decorated with crimson forests, blazing lava rivers, and fields of dark purple. She had to admit it was macabrely beautiful. Not that she'd ever want to live here. "We could follow the lava. As long as we keep it on our right as we retrace our steps, we'll end up in the glade."

Rajah shoved the useless compass away. "Obviously. That's just what I was going to suggest. Now do you want to waste more time or shall we get on with our quest?"

How much more did they have to climb? The slope seemed never-ending. But the bastion was somewhere on the other side, so up they continued, seeking handholds among the rocks, clinging onto branches or shinnying up the dangling vines. She had no idea how much time they spent ascending, but eventually Rajah stopped at a broad ledge with a sigh. "We'll rest here."

She sat down with relief. "Did anyone pack any food?"

Rajah frowned. "Pal?"

Pal shook his head. "I thought Faith had the food."

"Why did you think that?" she asked.

Rajah jumped up. "Neither of you? What is the point of having servants if they won't actually serve?"

Why did Pal just take the abuse? He sat there, head bowed, as Rajah rained down insults. She thought he'd stop after the first, lengthy tirade, but Rajah merely gasped for breath before launching into another barrage.

"Enough, Rajah," said Faith.

He stared at her. "What did you say?"

They glared at each other. She could be pushed only so far, and Rajah could take only so much humiliation. She wouldn't back down, but fighting out here wasn't in anyone's interests. So Faith allowed herself to relax. "We're in this together."

That was the opening Rajah needed to save his own face.

"Well, *obviously*. It's a good thing one of us is prepared. I found these back in the glade."

He delved into his rucksack and took out a neatly folded parcel. Laying it on the ground before them, he opened up the folds. "Mushrooms. They'll make a wonderful stew."

Faith gazed at them. "I thought nothing edible grew in the Nether. It was all poisonous."

"Not these," said Rajah. Then he popped one in his mouth.

Faith waited for him to turn purple, or erupt with yellow boils. But Rajah chewed, a fresh smile spreading. "Cook used these in her special recipe. The mushrooms only grew in the Nether, so we only served it for our most important guests. She swore me to secrecy, but I know the recipe. There's enough here for all of us."

How about that? Rajah cooked for them! The mushrooms were turned to paste in the bowl, a few herbs sprinkled in, water from his canteen, and then held over a hastily constructed fire. Soon they were tucking into Rajah's meal. And it was *delicious*.

Rajah did have a talent after all.

The tiredness just fell away. Faith saw it on the others' faces. Pal picked at it cautiously until he took his first spoonful, then devoured it, shaking his head in wonder. Rajah was good at something. Really good.

Rajah ate with a faraway look and a faint, wistful smile. Food did that, didn't it? It reminded us of better times, and there were few things better than sitting in a circle sharing a meal. But soon, too soon, the bowls were empty and packed away.

Faith peered up at the slope. It was steeper, but it didn't matter. Fresh strength flowed through her body. "That was some soup, Rajah."

"Thanks," he said. "But that's Sir Rajah."

"Of course." She gave a curtsy. "Most gracious of you, Sir Rajah."

Rajah cleared his throat. "I'll lead."

"Can you hear that?" Rajah paused upon the slope. He peered at the ridge ahead.

Faith turned to listen. "Sounds like . . . fighting?"

"Come on," said the knight, unhooking his axe.

They crawled the final distance, pausing briefly as they heard distant shouts, screams, and the echo of steel upon steel. And there were other, stranger sounds.

"Is that squealing?" asked Faith.

"Maybe there's a farm nearby?" suggested Pal.

"Sounds like a miserable kind of farm if the animals are making that racket." She slid her fingers along the bowstring till she found the sweet spot. "What are they doing to those poor pigs?"

Rajah stood at the top of the ridge. "You need to see this for yourselves."

"See what?" she asked, lumbering up beside him.

"I . . . I can't really describe it."

They'd reached the top. The slope descended to a deep, broad valley dominated by a vast, crumbling keep of grim, forbidding blackstone. A vast, crumbling keep surrounded by a moat of lava. Upon the single-arched bridge that spanned the moat was a horde of armored figures battling another group.

Faith rubbed her eyes. "I must be more tired than I thought. They look like pigs in armor."

"That's because they *are* pigs in armor," said Pal. "Piglins."

Faith shook her head. "I thought you were joking."

Pal turned his attention toward the band the piglins were fighting. "And that other group? Recognize the guy at the front?"

She did. "Tyrus. The Mapmaker was right, the Bravos came through their own portal. Now what?"

They both turned around to Rajah. This was his quest, this was his call.

He stood there, staring with wide-eyed fear at the battle. Armored pigs and the Bravos: not a great combination to instill confidence. He was probably still remembering how Heartbreaker shattered. Was it only yesterday? How many more things can go wrong within a day? She knew the quest was over. No way was Rajah brave enough to face—

"I'm not letting the Bravos steal my glory," said Rajah, tightening his hold on his axe. "Let the swine fight it out. We're going in."

How about that? Maybe there was a kernel of courage deep under that spoiled exterior.

"We need to find another way in," she said. "The Bravos and the piglins look like they're going to be busy for a while on that bridge."

The bastion was immense. The towers rose to dizzying heights and the walls looked impenetrable. And then there was the not-inconsiderable challenge of the moat. The lava bubbled and flames licked the surface, pitting the bottom-most section of the wall. And from their high vantage point they could see into the courtyards and squares beyond the perimeter wall and glimpse the other mobs that lurked within the bastion remnants.

"We're going to have to be sneaky," said Pal. "In, grab the loot, and straight out. Agreed?"

Faith nodded. Sneaky suited her just fine.

Rajah chewed his lip. "My father never sneaked in his whole life. His armor was made of diamonds. You could see him coming from over the horizon. He'd be there." Rajah pointed at the bridge. "Right at the front, swinging Heartbreaker and having pork chops for tea."

What was he suggesting? They fight alongside the Bravos?

Rajah looked at his axe. Plain and simple and made of stone. "He'd never have fought with a weapon like this. It would have been beneath him."

Pal looked at his master sympathetically. "Sire, this is—"

Rajah stood up. He shrugged and settled the axe in his hands. "But there are many paths to glory. I'm tired of trying to follow my father's. It's time I found my own." He looked back at them. "So let's go grab all the glory while no one's looking."

CHAPTER 8

LAVA POURED DOWN FROM above. Faith's skin crawled with the knowledge of how far they were from the world they knew. The air was hot and stagnant. There were no fresh breezes, just an oppressive heat. Vast pools of lava bubbled all around, and the vegetation was strange fungi; some glowed while others were as tall as trees. Walls of flame crackled in the distance and obscured the horizon in a heat haze. Sweat steamed from her brow as she struggled onward.

The lands around the bastion remnant included patches of forest, so they approached undetected. They passed a shimmering portal, with the remains of previous adventurers scattered among the roots and patches of foliage. For some, their quest had not ended well.

Their gear lay abandoned. Most had rusted or rotted away, though if they'd wanted, they could have rearmed. But it was hard taking a sword from the skeletal grip of its previous owner.

"No one thinks it'll happen to them," said Pal. "That's the

human condition, I suppose. Despite all the odds, we think we'll be the ones who win the big prize. Poor fools."

"You don't think we're up to it?" she asked.

"What I think doesn't matter. It's all up to him."

Rajah walked among the skeletal remains, more somber than she was used to. What was he thinking? That those hollowed skulls had once been filled with the same dreams as his? Was there a crack opening up in his mighty wall of arrogance?

But was that what they needed right now? A sense of doom? "Rajah? Why? He's a decent fella, but he's a fool. No disrespect intended."

Pal frowned at her. "I promised I'd look out for him. I have a reason to be here, you don't. Not sure who's the bigger fool, him, or you for following him."

"I thought it would be an adventure," said Faith. "You'd understand if you'd grown up where I did."

"Let me guess. Every day was like the last. You knew everyone in your village. You were going to do exactly what your parents had done, and they'd done the same as their parents. Your mom married the first guy she kissed."

"So you've been there?" Faith asked. She guessed most small villages were the same. That was the problem.

"Everyone looked out for one another. Shared the good times, supported one another during the bad. Neighbors helped rebuild the wall when a creeper blew it up. Food on the table, without fail. Fell asleep gazing at the flames in the hearth, right? All tucked in and safe. A boring life, but a safe one."

How could she explain it to him? The stagnation? The insular world she'd been raised in? Sure, everyone helped one another, but strangers? The fear? The distrust? Not just of outsiders, but of any idea that wasn't already covered in cobwebs. You can be a living, breathing being, but you could still be dead inside, lifeless through and through. That's why she'd had to go. No one else had understood her desire, her passion for change. They feared change. Most people did. Why? She'd seen people who lived miserable lives but were too scared to do anything about it. People chose familiarity over happiness. She wasn't going to be like that. "There's hope in the future."

Pal shook his head, then plodded on after Rajah.

Choices. That was the difference between their lives. Pal didn't have any. It didn't matter how great your life was, if you'd not chosen it, one way or another, it would be a prison. She missed home, but this was where she belonged, this was her life, not the one that had been laid out by her parents, and their parents, and going all the way back to the first person who'd settled in that patch of ground and planted the first seed.

The bastion rose from the somber darkness. A vast, sprawling monolith of blackstone and lava falls. The fiery streams poured into the moat surrounding the great castle, splashing against the scorched bank. A blackstone bridge spanned the moat, its edges cracked by the intense heat, and beyond was a set of doors, wide open. And through them poured strange, hybrid creatures. They could have been human, at first glance, but they had pig heads. They'd formed a crowd and were fighting the Bravos as they tried to force their way in. Arrows darted back and forth between the two parties, locked in a scrum, each trying to force the other back. In the center of the battle, waving his huge axe over his head, hacking at the pig creatures, was Tyrus.

"The Bravos are certainly living up to their name," said Pal. "It's pretty brave to battle your way through the front gates."

"Pretty stupid, too," said Faith. "What are those creatures called again?"

"Piglins," said Rajah. "Nasty creatures. Father tried cooking one once. Not as tasty as you'd imagine."

The sounds of the battle echoed across the cavernous kingdom. Tyrus and his Bravos yelled their war cry, and the piglins snorted and squealed. Weapons hammered against shields. The din of clashing steel was unrelenting.

"Should we go and help?" she asked. "The Bravos look like they're in trouble."

"Good," said Rajah.

"They don't need help, they need to retreat." Pal scanned the bastion. "Throwing ourselves into the melee will only make things worse. The Bravos might even attack us. They're the typical 'hack first, ask questions later' type of team."

Rajah sighed wistfully. "They were Father's favorite. He was old-school. He believed in the direct approach to adventuring. Simplistic, even."

"Which was what?" she asked. She knew she was new to all this, so some tips never hurt.

"Kick the door down, kill the monsters, and steal the treasure," said Rajah. "When you break it down to its most basic components, that's all there is to it."

"No one's kicking that door down," said Pal, pointing at the main gates. "The piglins are getting reinforcements. The Bravos really should run away while they can."

"But it's the only way in," said Rajah.

"Is it?" He wasn't so sure. The bastion was a ruin. A solid ruin, well defended and protected by a lava-filled moat, but that didn't mean there weren't options. "Let's scout around."

Faith remained watching the battle at the main gate. "Shouldn't we help?"

"Two questions: Why? And how?"

"It just doesn't feel right. In the stories the heroes always band together to defeat a great evil, setting aside their differences and celebrating victory by becoming blood brothers and sisters forevermore."

"I can see how that would make a better story than what really usually happens when two parties arrive at the same treasure."

She frowned, already sensing this wasn't going to be the answer she was hoping for. "Which is?"

"Rob each other. Usually violently."

Rajah nodded. "Pal's right, you know. Often was the time that Father would lie in wait for another party of heroes to return from their great quest, ambush them, and steal all their hard-won treasure."

"That's appalling," said Faith.

There was an overgrown path that seemed to circle the moat. As good a route as any. "Shall we get a move on?"

They crept around the perimeter, keeping with the vegetation. Pal had never seen anything like it. No trees, just the giant fungi, deep blue. He picked at the trunk, and it was as solid as any wood. The vines, too, were strong as rope. And how wide was the moat? The distance across varied, certainly too wide to jump, but could some bridge be laid across it? It wouldn't be more than a ladder, but find the right spot and they could get to the bastion walls. All they needed was—

"An opening." Faith pointed to a section of wall. "See? There's a crack in the wall. Wide enough for someone to squeeze through."

"Why haven't they repaired it?" asked Rajah.

Pal stood at the edge of the moat. The lava bubbled below, flames licking the sides of the moat. The air hissed all around them, shimmering with the intense heat. "Why bother? You'd have to be mad to try to cross here."

"Then what are we going to do?"

He slapped the trunk of the giant blue fungus. "We're going to cross here."

Rajah stepped way back from the edge. Waaay back. "That's . . . madness!"

"What's madness is us being here, and yet here we are. And that goes double for trying to do what the Bravos are doing. These trunks will hold, sire. Lash them together and we have ourselves a bridge across the moat. With any luck we'll be in and out while the piglins are still fighting Tyrus and his gang. It's the only way we can get in. You have to trust me."

"Trust you?" cried Rajah.

"Your father did, when he asked me to be your squire. Asked me to look out for you."

"And that's been working so well, hasn't it?" Rajah turned to the fiery moat, then back to Pal. "Are you absolutely sure?"

Absolutely . . . not. But they were desperate, and they were out of options. "I'll cross first."

Rajah drew his axe. "I'd better get used to using this. How many do you need?"

"Just the one. I should get seven pieces out of it. That'll do the job."

Rajah got chopping while Faith kept lookout. It was as if they were working as a team, finally. He watched Rajah sweat, and there were moments when his master looked like he was going to throw it all in. The fungi trunk was tougher than it looked, but who did he have to whine to? No one. That, more than any other reason, drove Rajah on. An honest day's labor, for once. The raw materials collected, they returned to the moat, and Pal got to work making his fungus bridge.

"I can't hear any fighting," said Faith. "You think the Bravos won?"

"If they did, they'll be the worse for wear. We can still do this, Faith." Pal gave the rung a good tug, to make sure. "This'll hold."

"Only one way to find out, isn't there?"

They lassoed the ends upon broken stubs on the ruined outer wall and then carefully rolled out the bridge. Now was the moment of truth. Would it hold?

Pal brushed his hands clean. "I built it so guess I'd better test it."

Pal stepped onto it, arms outspread, letting the first plank take his weight. The ladder began to bow, the fungus creaking ominously. The lava bubbled with excitement, as if it could sense him.

The closer he got to the middle, the more it swayed. He should have turned back; now it was too late. Could he jump to the opposite side from here, if it gave way? It seemed too far. Maybe one more step. But that step would create more of a bend, maybe too much. The whole thing would snap. That's what it was going to do, if he took another step. But he couldn't go backward, either, not without turning around.

"Slowly," said Faith. "And spread the weight out."

The heat was unbearable. Sweat hissed off his skin. Through the haze he saw the opposite side, safety, just a little ahead of him.

He grabbed the vines and steadied himself and then, step by

wary step, Pal began to cross, eyes locked on the far edge. The vines creaked as he approached, but his weight was working for him, settling the vines into their knots a little deeper. Finally he reached the far end and was up by the wall.

"Pal?" shouted Faith. "Are you okay?"

He wiped the sweat away. "Nothing to it."

Faith went across next, swiftly, hardly looking down, and he grabbed her the moment she was in reach. She stared at the fiery crevasse, then grinned. "Another one off the bucket list."

"You are mad if you enjoyed that," he said.

She turned to face Rajah. "It's fine. Just don't look down!"

Rajah peered over the edge and gulped. "What if I fall?"

"You won't. Trust me." Pal held out his hand. "I'll catch you at this end."

There they stood facing each other over an expanse where one misstep meant death. How much did you trust someone with your life? They'd grown up together—the few years between them hadn't mattered when they'd been younger—and knew each other better than brothers, but as time went on the differences became more noticeable. Rajah was son of a lord, Pal merely his servant, there to prop him up. But Pal wanted Rajah to succeed, wanted to see him triumph over his doubts, his inbuilt sense of being a failure, the unworthy son.

"You can do it," said Pal.

He hesitated. He peered down into the lava, his stark, terrified face lit by the hellish glow. There were a dozen steps between them. All Rajah needed to do was take them and he'd be a different man, he'd be one step closer to becoming the hero he dreamed about. Heroes weren't fearless; they felt fear as strongly and deeply as everyone else. But they conquered it and went on regardless.

Rajah just needed a little . . . push.

"Fine. We'll come back over and go to the Mapmaker and tell him we couldn't find the netherite. He'll understand. I wonder who he'll sell the map to?"

Faith played along. "Tyrus, of course. I'm sure he and his party will be heading off to Castle Redstone tomorrow morning. We'll be hearing that tale from every bard we meet for the rest of our lives. I doubt they'll be singing about anyone else after that."

Pal nodded. "He'll be the most famous hero in the realm *ever*."

"No, he will not," snarled Rajah.

He came across fast, and screaming. They both caught him as he tripped on the last plank, his foot flailing through the gap. A sudden gout of flame leapt up from below, as if there were fiery imps trying to catch him, to claim at least one. But they hung on and pulled Rajah up beside them.

"I did it," he whispered to himself, gazing back at the moat.

They'd all done it, but Pal was happy to let Rajah have his moment of pride. And why not? He had so few.

They tried to lift the ladder back up but it had gotten wedged in and would have to stay. How long would it last? The flames would work on it, weakening its structure quickly enough. If they wanted to go out this way, they needed to be quick. Pal drew out his pickaxe and peered into the crack in the wall. It took a few moments to adjust to the gloom, but there was light, at least a glow, ahead.

Okay, this was scary. Proper delving-deep-into-nightmares territory. Not so much trying to break into a heavily defended bastion as being in charge. The worst part was that everyone was acting like they were counting on him so, despite having no idea what to do next, Pal turned to them and said, "Follow me."

It was easier to leave the decisions to others, even if they were fools. People liked to be led, have others tell them how to run their lives. He knew better than most. Now? Just when they needed a proper hero to take charge, it was down to him. Pal's grip on his pickaxe was so tight, it trembled. He squeezed through the opening, ears straining for the sound of any porcine activity.

The crack though the wall opened up. Light from flickering torches illuminated a dank, narrow corridor. The others emerged behind him. Faith's determination didn't hide her own nervousness, while Rajah stared around, wide-eyed, amazed he'd made it this far.

They explored, one behind the other, keeping quiet, but the bastion was a big place. "Where do you think the treasure room would be?"

"At the heart of the citadel," said Rajah. "We need to venture farther into—"

Pal clapped his hand over Rajah's mouth. Faith fell silent and the three of them pressed themselves against the wall and into the shadows.

The sound of armored footsteps grew louder. Someone was coming their way.

They'd get only one chance. They needed to take the wanderer out in a single moment; otherwise they'd raise the alarm and the whole escapade would be over. He just hoped he knew the way back to the wall opening.

A large shadow fell upon the opposite wall. The footsteps grew louder. Pal saw the armored figure come around the corner.

"Now!" he yelled.

His pickaxe clanged upon a shield, and he was bashed aside, slammed back against the wall with the air knocked out of him.

Rajah swung his axe but the target ducked nimbly under it, despite the heavy armor. Faith's arrow bounced harmlessly off the breastplate, and then the bow was knocked from her hand. The figure raised his axe and stepped into the torchlight. "You lot are dead! You think you can get the drop on Tyrus?"

Tyrus?

Oh no.

With a wild, manic glint in his eyes, Tyrus raised his axe to finish Pal off.

CHAPTER 9

AND THEN RAJAH LEAPT in front of him. "Tyrus! Stop!"

He did, but barely. The blow would have split Rajah's head wide open but Tyrus twisted at the last moment and the axe skated down the stone wall, trailing screaming sparks behind it.

The knight stared at them, dumbfounded. "What . . . how did you get in here?"

He looked battered. His armor, so bright and shiny only yesterday, was dented and scorched. He wore a bandage around his forehead, and his left eye was swollen. But his grip on his axe was steady, and the fire in his eyes was a warning.

"It's not just you who goes on quests," said Rajah.

Tyrus grabbed Rajah by the collar. "I don't believe it! Have you been following me?"

"Let go of him," snapped Faith, pulling Rajah free. "We found our own way in. Whether you like it or not, we're in this together."

Tyrus snarled and for a moment Faith thought he was going to launch into them. The guy wanted to fight everything! He even kept flexing his fingers around his axe haft. "Stay out of my way," snarled Tyrus. "Or I'm going to leave you to the piglins."

"Where's the rest of your party?" asked Faith.

Tyrus shook his head. "I'm on my own."

What else had he expected? He'd thought they could barge in through the front door. What was it about heroes? They thought the story was all about them. But Pal saw the pain in Tyrus's face. He'd been the leader and let them down. "Join us."

"What?" said Tyrus.

"What?" said Rajah.

"We need all the help we can get." Pal faced the unconvinced Tyrus. "And that goes double for you. We're in the bastion now, but we still need to find the treasure room and we still need to get out. Whatever we've faced already, we've got to assume we'll be facing mobs just as bad on the way back."

Rajah scratched his beard. "That's a cheery thought. I hadn't considered problems with the journey back."

Of course he hadn't. Rajah's eyes were always on the prize, never on the chores. They had a long slog ahead, unless . . .

Pal peered at Tyrus. "Where's your portal?"

Tyrus scowled. "That's none of your business."

"It's near, isn't it? That's why you beat us here. Ours is way on the other side of the valley ridge, but yours is just beyond the bastion. It must be."

"Like I said, it's none of your business. I'm not telling you where my portal is."

Stubborn and stupid. But then Pal was used to that. It seemed to be an essential part of a hero's personality. "Then we're not going to tell you how we got in. Good luck on getting back out the same way you came in. Those piglins must have gathered a whole army at the gates by now. You going to hack your way through all of them?"

Tyrus glowered. "If I have to."

Stubborn, stupid, and suicidal.

How could he get through to him? How could he make sense penetrate that iron helmet and the even denser skull under it? "If this is about the treasure, there'll be more than enough for all of us. We'll split it four ways."

"The treasure doesn't matter. This is about the glory. I'm not having you steal it from me when I've done all the hard work. You call yourselves heroes?"

"Actually we don't. We're just—"

But Tyrus wasn't listening. "Lord Maharajah had a party, too, didn't he? He didn't go in alone on his escapades and quests. There were others with him, but who remembers them?"

Rajah nodded. "They all sort of blended into one. He just used to refer to them as 'Harry.' So?"

Tyrus pointed at each of them. "So who will the bards and minstrels sing about? You can share treasure, but glory? It's all or nothing."

"Then you'd better get used to nothing," said Faith.

They all turned to look at her, expressions varying from aghast (from Rajah), to anger (from Tyrus), to Pal's own quiet amusement.

Tyrus stepped right up to her, nose-to-nose. "Who are you, again?"

Then, surprisingly, Rajah squeezed himself between them. "She's with *us*."

"Fine. We'll join forces." Tyrus adjusted his armor. He did that thing warriors do with their weapons, that strange wrist spin. "But we never, ever talk about this when we get back. Agreed?"

"Who'd believe us anyway," said Pal.

"Exactly," said Tyrus. "Tyrus working with the likes of you? Laughable."

Which way now? Pal picked a corridor that he was pretty certain was heading west, deeper into the heart of the bastion, the most likely location for the treasure room. "Now's not the time for heroism."

Faith frowned at him. "What about the ghast I roasted? What would you call that then?"

"I call that you doing your job. Brave, sure. Clever, yes. Heroic? If that makes you feel better. But my point still stands. No use going looking for trouble. Sooner or later it'll find you anyway."

Pal took the lead. He had a knack for finding his way, indoors and out. It was probably all those years working in the manor, scurrying around on a thousand errands, exploring every nook and cranny in Lord Maharajah's ramshackle home. He'd loved it there. But it turned out everyone designed castles the same way, more or less. If you've explored one, you've explored them all. They hid from snorting piglin patrols, crept past the stables with their rooting hoglins, and were forced to cross more than one lava pit. But the deeper they went, the grander and more elaborate the bastion became. They crossed a vast blackstone hall lit by lava fountains, and a bridge across a smoking void where the wind carried mournful whispers.

But eventually they entered a long hall, the floor decorated with patterns of different blocks. At the far end stood a pair of huge iron doors.

"This must be it, the doors built by the Mapmaker's old long-gone rival," said Pal. "The treasure room is beyond."

Rajah put his shoulder against one door. "Help me, then."

They all pushed. No luck.

Faith rubbed her shoulder. "There might be another way in."

Pal stepped back for a better look at it. "Maybe, but it could take ages finding it. We're right here, Faith. There must be a way to open the doors."

They were so close! There had to be a way to open the doors. But if there was nothing on the doors themselves . . .

Faith's gaze dropped to the floor. "Why these patterns? The rest of the bastion is just plain blackstone. Look at these. Wood. Stone. Obsidian. Lapis lazuli. Even gold. And they're all connected by some red powder. Mean anything to you?"

"They must be pressure plates." Pal rubbed his fingers upon the red dust. They tingled. "There's something here."

"Redstone dust," said Rajah. "What else could it be? My father talked about the strange circuits he came across on his quest to find Castle Redstone."

It was making sense. "These red lines are binding the design together into activating some . . . mechanism?"

Rajah gestured at the blocks—pressure plates—decorating the floor. "You just need to press the right one and the door will open. It's obvious."

Pal frowned. "And if you press the wrong one?"

Faith arched an eyebrow. "Something bad happens?"

Rajah sighed. "It usually does. So the doors are a trap."

But what sort of trap? He stood before the door, gazing at the flagstones, the ceiling, the sidewalls. There was no way to deactivate it, not without digging all around the doors, looking for the mechanism that controlled it. If you couldn't deactivate the trap you only had one other option, didn't you? He started retreating from the door. "We need to set it off."

"What do you think'll happen?" asked Faith.

"Either nothing at all, or something to do with lava. If I was designing this, I'd have the floor collapse the moment anyone pressed the gold panel. There's a whole lake of lava under this building, so pit fall makes the most sense." He gestured to the far wall. "We'll be safe over there. Then I want you to shoot an arrow at the wooden pressure plate."

Tyrus struck his axe against his shield. "This is wasting time. The piglins will be sniffing out our trail."

Rajah headed for the far wall. "Your trail, you mean?"

Was he right? He'd look an idiot if nothing happened. Then better seem an idiot than be burned alive in lava. That was the great thing about people having low expectations about you. Failure was expected.

Faith drew the bowstring to her ear, and loosed.

The arrow struck dead-center with a satisfying deep thunk before scuttling across the floor. The noise echoed on, but that was it.

Tyrus laughed. "That's what happens when you start taking advice from your servants. There's a reason why it's best not to let them think too—"

The floor started sliding open. The temperature suddenly skyrocketed as the heat from the lava revealed below rose into the room. In a matter of moments there'd be no way to reach the door.

Faith grabbed a handful of arrows. "Get ready to run!"

"We'll never make it!" cried Rajah.

"Just be ready!" she shot again, hitting another pressure plate dead-center. Another section of the floor started sliding open.

"That is not helping," said Pal.

"Oh? Please feel free to offer any advice!"

He grabbed her hand before she shot again. "Wait."

"We don't have—"

"Wait."

Pal analyzed the circuits. The two that Faith had hit had matching designs. So it made sense that the rest with the same designs activated the same mechanism, withdrawing the floor sections. So that meant . . .

He pointed at a wooden block on the top right, nearest the door. "That one."

"How do you know?"

"Different design. Different function. It has to be."

With a nod Faith loosed her arrow.

Hidden pistons came alive. The doors shuddered, then slid open.

Faith smirked. "Not bad, Pal. Not bad at all."

In spite of himself, he smiled back. "Save the celebrations until we're out of here."

Tyrus grinned, his eyes bright with greed. "Let's grab the treasure."

Then, even as the floor sections continued to open up, they ran.

CHAPTER 10

THE TREASURE ROOM HAD been built upon a pool of lava; the only way across were bridges that crisscrossed the deadly expanse toward a central platform. Faith gestured ahead through the infernal, shimmering heat to a large chest. "They're just sitting there. But it's all too easy."

"Too easy? I lost my entire party getting in here." Tyrus raised his axe. "I'm getting what's owed."

"Hang on. We need to be careful. Do you honestly think the treasure would be left undefended?"

"But I don't see anything."

"Exactly," she said. "There's some last trap, I know it."

"How? How do you know it? You ever been in the Nether before. Or explored a bastion."

"No, but that doesn't mean—"

He smiled. It was patronizing and superior. "Why don't you leave this to the experts, then? You just wait here and let me take care of things, eh?"

"Don't you get it? I'm trying to help you!"

"I do not need the help of a little girl like you. I'm Sir Tyrus, remember? My name's famous across the whole realm! Now just sit quietly and watch how a real hero does it."

He was worse than Rajah. Was there some rule about heroes being arrogant noobs she didn't know about? "Fine. Show me."

Tyrus flicked his hair with a huff. He glowered at each of them, as if daring any to help him. The guy was a fool.

Rajah leaned against the wall and searched his pockets for a snack. "Don't be too long. I can smell sweaty pork."

Tyrus crept across the bridge, axe tightly gripped, his eyes narrowed to the thinnest of slits. The torches flickered, casting undulating shadows across the floor. The only sound was the clink of Tyrus's armor.

And nothing happened.

She'd expected something. A spear to shoot out from a hidden nook, or the floor to open up over a pool of lava, but Tyrus crossed the chamber without incident.

"Well, that's stupid," she declared. "Who'd build a treasure room and not put any traps inside it?"

"Shall we go join him?" said Rajah. "He'll get dibs on the good stuff, I suppose. It's the honorable thing to do."

Honorable but, in her opinion, stupid. "Shouldn't it all be divided equally?"

Rajah laughed. "Only among equals! Tyrus first, then me, then Pal, then you. That's the pecking order of life."

"Why do I go last? Is it because I'm a novice or for another reason?"

Rajah gazed at her, startled. "Like what?"

"I know the stories. The women are only in them as damsels in need of rescuing. Women never get to be heroes."

Pal stifled a laugh. "I think you've disproved that already."

Faith scowled. "There's a long way still to go."

"Come on! It's perfectly safe!" yelled Tyrus as he stood with one foot resting on the treasure chest. "Just as I predicted."

They crossed the nearest bridge, Faith careful to step only where Tyrus had stepped. There still might be a pressure pad among the flagstones . . .

But they all gathered at the chest without anything being set off, exploding, opening up, or being launched at them. She was sincerely disappointed. "Now what?"

Tyrus wrapped both hands around his axe haft. "We smash the chest open and steal whatever's inside. Step back a bit, I wouldn't want you hurt by any splinters."

But there was something else. "Wait. Can you smell that? There's something burning. Maybe we should check the chest a little more care —"

Tyrus swung his axe over his shoulder with a roar, smashing the heavy padlock off the chest. He smirked at her and kicked the chest over.

The contents scattered over the floor. Ingots of gold and iron bounced off in all directions, but they weren't what they'd come for. Among the gold and iron were ingots of black metal, chill to the touch despite the surrounding heat.

Tyrus gestured to the rock. "I'll take the netherite."

"There are six pieces. We could go halves."

He shook his head. "No. It's all mine. You can have the loose change. Buy yourself a real weapon, Rajah. You look ridiculous with that stone axe. How do you think your father would react seeing you running around, armed like some caveman?"

But that burning smell was getting stronger. Where was it coming from? She looked over at Pal. "I smell it, too. We need to leave."

Tyrus scoffed. "Run away, little chickens."

The air shimmered, blowing a strong, hot breeze across the treasure room. A small, smoldering cube appeared, rising up through the bubbling lava. It began to expand, flames licking across its surface. The room swelled with firelight.

"No good at all," said Rajah, backing away.

Lava dripped from the cube, leaving hissing puddles upon the flagstones. The hissing grew louder, the heat intensifying moment by moment.

"We need to get out," she said.

Tyrus stared at the fiery mass. "I'm not running. Never have, never will."

What was the guy trying to prove? Was he really that desperate to have a heroic death?

The cube filled the center of the chamber. Its eyes opened, two holes filled with blazing fires. It turned slowly, great drops of lava dripping from its body. The air surrounding it trembled with the heat.

"Magma cube," whispered Rajah. "My father fought one, once. A single cube should be no problem."

Pal groaned as he gestured to more glowing shapes emerging from the hidden corners of the treasure room. "How about three?"

Rajah took a faltering step backward. "Ah. That requires an entirely different strategy."

Hands shaking, Faith nocked an arrow. It seemed a ridiculously feeble weapon against the burning entity closing in. "Which is?"

Rajah gulped before answering. "Run."

CHAPTER 11

PAL SHOVED THE NETHERITE into his rucksack and slung it over his back. It was heavy, but a good heavy. "Let's go before trouble finds us."

Rajah thumbed his axe. "But what about Tyrus?"

"Not our problem."

"But he'll die."

"Refer to my previous comment." Pal started toward the door, then realized neither Rajah nor Faith was following him. "Come on, then."

Rajah tightened his grip on his haft. "I was just thinking . . ."

Uh-oh. Rajah thinking was never a good sign.

". . . but what would my father do?"

"Not got himself in this mess in the first place?" It wasn't the best answer, but it was an honest one. "Let me remind you that Tyrus really didn't want to come along with us."

The three magma cubes had spread out across the chamber, working together to corral them into a corner. If they didn't run now, then they'd risk being incinerated from all directions.

Faith stepped alongside Rajah. "That was then, this is now."

He could see what they were wanting to do, which just happened to be the complete opposite of what he wanted. "They're magma cubes. How in the Creator's name are we going to defeat three of them?"

Faith smiled at him. "We'll think of something. We always do."

"That's not true on any level," he moaned, but neither was listening. They just wanted to go do hero stuff.

And they weren't waiting. They ran toward the cubes. He could just go without them. He had the treasure, after all, and wasn't that the entire reason they were here?

Pal was about to shout after them but they were gone.

He drew out his pickaxe and raced after them. He could feel the bridge shaking from the cube's bounds.

He caught up with them at the corner. Rajah's eyes were bright with excitement while Faith had an arrow nocked. She tilted her head toward the sound of battle. "Concentrate on one at a time, starting with the one in the middle. We'll surprise it and hit it as hard as we can, as quickly as we can. Keep it simple, all right?"

"After you," said Pal, hoping they didn't hear the resentment.

They didn't. Faith nodded at them and turned the corner, Rajah a step behind her. Then he raised his axe and charged.

One magma cube hopped after Tyrus, each impact making the whole room shake. Tyrus ducked behind a pillar as the thing smashed into it and barely managed to get away from the falling debris. He hadn't even noticed them.

Faith launched a volley at the first magma cube's rear as Rajah charged it. The arrows pierced its hide and the creature spun toward this fresh threat. Rajah swung his axe and the magma cube shuddered. Pal yelled and attacked the third magma cube, doing everything he could just to stay out of reach by running away as often as he could.

Tyrus took a moment to gather his breath then, seeing the odds suddenly improved, pressed on with his own onslaught.

Working together, Rajah and Faith landed blow after blow on the mob even as arrows struck it and the magma cube trembled violently. It bounded high toward Faith; she had nowhere to flee. If it landed on her—

The arrow struck it mid-leap. The magma cube burst apart . . .

. . . into four smaller cubes. They bounced and bounded off in all directions, chasing after the others. One crashed into Rajah, sending him spinning across the room.

A moment later the second magma cube erupted apart into another cluster of smaller cubes.

How was this helping? They were everywhere!

Pal ducked behind a column to hide from the last of the larger cubes. They needed another plan. But what?

Pal took out a pinch of gunpowder. He watched the cubes, seeing how they jumped and crashed against walls and other obstacles. That was it . . .

He snatched the bag of gunpowder and the sack of sand off his belt. The others had joined together to destroy the final large cube; it, too, had fragmented, and now there were a dozen smaller cubes leaping and bouncing in all directions, trailing lava in their wake. One smashed into Faith, almost flattening her against the wall. She couldn't take another battering like that.

Pal scooped the sand into a pile by the doorway. Was that enough? Too much? No way of knowing, no time to test it out. He reached into his backpack and pulled out his crafting table, slamming it hard onto the floor.

Rajah glanced over at him. "You have to do that now? *Really?*"

"Just give me a few moments, sire! I have an idea!"

"An idea? Let me share mine with you. Run!"

"Not this time," Pal snapped. "This is going to work."

Probably.

Most likely?

If they were lucky?

Pal then grabbed a handful of gunpowder and threw it on.

There. That seemed right. Now all he needed was a catalyst . . . "Faith! I need to light this up!"

"Light what? What is it?"

"Our escape plan!" he yelled. "Just give it some heat!"

Faith nodded, then aimed her arrow as another magma cube bounced toward her. Her arrow passed beneath it, through the lava dripping from its body. The shaft caught alight instantly and the flaming arrow arced over them like a comet.

"Come on! Run!" he yelled. They needed to get out right now. One eye on the battle, the other on the burning pile, he knew they had only moments.

Rajah swatted aside a magma cube and raced for the door while Faith loosed arrows to give cover, but Tyrus stubbornly battled on.

"What are you doing?" cried Pal. "Get out of here!"

Tyrus merely tightened his grip on his axe. "I do not run."

"Then you're going to get trapped here. And no one will hear your tale, Tyrus. A sad, lonely end. Is that what you want? To be forgotten?"

Tyrus glowered. Pal could almost feel the heat of his blood boiling. He just needed to raise its temperature a little higher . . .

"The Great Sir Rajah. That's who they'll be singing about.

How he ventured into the Nether and conquered a bastion all by himself. And who'll be there to say otherwise?"

"Never," snarled Tyrus. "I'll not have that whelp steal my glory."

Pal smirked. "Better get a move on, then."

And for the first time in his career, Tyrus ran.

"You'd better know what you're doing," said Faith.

Not exactly, but he wasn't about to share that detail with her. Pal threw in that last handful of gunpowder.

Thick smoke was rising from the mixture, which was about to go critical. Faith picked up her pace and threw herself through the doorway, knocking them both over and out of the treasure room.

The explosion devastated the entire doorway. The lintel crashed down along with half the ceiling. Rajah grabbed his arm and hauled him up. "That was madness, Pal."

The magma cubes crashed against the debris that now filled in the doorway. He'd trapped them on the other side.

"How did you know that was the right amount?" asked Faith.

"I didn't."

"You could have blown yourself up."

"That was no more a risk than the one you were taking." He shook off the worst of the dust. "Now can we finally get out of here?"

They ran along the corridor, leaving the chaos of the treasure room battle behind them. "You're enjoying this?" he asked Faith.

She grinned. "And you're not? We did it, Pal! We did it!"

It had been terror from start to finish, and it wasn't finished yet. They still needed to get out of here. They stopped around a corner to gather their breath. Tyrus's skin was red, his hair singed and steaming with sweat. He'd lost his axe somehow and his shield was fire-blackened—burned through in places. "How do we get out, Tyrus? Where's your portal?"

"It's no use, we'll never get past the piglins. They'll have reinforced the main gate by now."

"We didn't come via the main gate."

Tyrus stared at him, bewildered. "There's no other way in. There's only one bridge across the moat."

"There're two now," said Rajah, slapping Pal on the back. "My servant built it. He's quite a clever fella."

As compliments went, that wasn't the worst. Not the best, but it would have to do, until a better one came along.

Faith turned the corner and joined them. "We've trapped the cubes but that bang you made will have every mob in the bastion coming to find out who caused it. Let's not hang around, eh?"

She wasn't getting any argument from him. Even Tyrus nodded. Pal supposed he was less keen on heroic last stands.

The piglins and hoglins came snorting and charging down the corridor. The hoglins were ahead, gaining speed as their trotters clattered upon the flagstones.

"Too many to fight," said Pal, already retreating. "We have what we came for, let's get to the bridge."

And surprisingly, no one argued with that, either.

The mobs chased them. The bastion had been invaded, and the piglins and hoglins wanted revenge. Pal could even smell the burning air that had escaped from the treasure room. The bastion had been in pretty bad condition already, though, so he doubted anyone would really notice a few more ruins.

They climbed through the rent in the outer wall to the fungus-and-vine bridge. It was smoking; small flames licked the underside, and the moisture within the fungi hissed and steamed.

Tyrus stared at it, and at the swirling lava below. "I'd rather take on the piglins."

"It's perfectly safe," said Pal. "Probably."

"Let's not dillydally." Rajah climbed up and ran across.

Faith turned to Pal. "Did he just say 'dillydally'?"

"He says a lot of stuff that makes no sense. That's because he's educated."

Faith crossed over, then, with great reluctance, Tyrus. He was halfway when the bridge creaked. He ran the rest, but his weight had weakened the trunk.

The piglins squealed as they saw Pal, and that signaled it was time for him to go. The flames curled around the planks and lashed at his ankles; the soles of his boots smoldered. The bridge swayed a lot and the vines were unraveling.

He'd built the bridge. It would hold just a little longer.

"Come on, Pal!" yelled Faith. "What are you waiting for?"

He glanced behind. The first piglin stepped up cautiously onto the bridge, the leader perhaps, while the others gathered behind, squealing encouragement. It glared at Pal and snorted as it swapped its sword from one hand to the next. The bridge was unstable enough with one person, but with two? Pal stepped on the next plank, ignoring the dizzying sensation as the bridge swung more and more. What if it flipped? He pushed that out of his mind and focused on the others waiting. Even Rajah looked worried. After all, who would fold his socks if not Pal?

Faith held out her hand. Pal went for it. He ran the final few planks, almost slipping on the last, but Faith and Rajah grabbed him and hauled him to the solid ground. The piglin leader squealed as it jumped from plank to plank while others piled onto the bridge behind it.

Pal held out his hand. "The axe."

The piglin's eyes widened with horror. It squealed in terror and started backing away, but others had clambered on behind it, and there was no retreat.

Pal swung. The ladder creaked and splintered. The other piglins squealed as the bridge began to shift. The lead piglin lowered its head as it ran straight for him, hopping from rung to rung.

The axe came down one more time and split the ladder. The ground gave way and the bridge began sliding downward. The piglin on it squealed one last time before it went tumbling into the lava.

The remaining piglins squealed in rage, but there was nothing they could do, not from the opposite side of the moat.

Rajah peered over the edge and licked his lips. "I don't know about you but I suddenly fancy some cooked pork chops."

CHAPTER 12

THE JOURNEY THROUGH THE portal was just as bad as the first. Faith's throat was sore from screaming, and by the time they stumbled back into the real world, the others looked just as shaken. Rajah went behind a tree to empty his guts, and Pal sat there hugging himself. "I'm never doing that again," he told her.

Tyrus faced them, hands on his hips. "I never thought I'd end up being saved by the likes of you. Remember, if anyone asks what happened, keep my name out of it."

Faith stood up and faced him. "Are you really so worried about your reputation?"

"That's all I've got. Taken me a long time to build it. Anyway, who would believe you? Tyrus being rescued by the likes of Rajah? As I said before, it's laughable."

"But it's true, that's exactly what happened."

"Since when did people believe the truth?" said Tyrus. "They believe the best stories. You'll realize that soon enough." His hand rested on the belt loop where his axe had hung, and he grimaced. "Guess I'll be starting over again."

"You could join us," Faith said. "There's room for a fourth."

Rajah returned, wiping his mouth. "That's not your decision. I'm the leader of this party, remember?" He adjusted the cuffs of his tunic. "So, Tyrus. Would you want to join our party? There's room for a fourth."

"But that's what I just said!"

Rajah frowned. "Did you? When?"

He genuinely did not remember. Wow, she'd known that nobles didn't see the world the way the rest of them did, but now she realized they didn't see the rest of the world at all.

Tyrus shook his head. "I'll see you around. And remember, if you tell anyone about what happened in the Nether, I'll deny it and, frankly, who'd believe you anyway?"

He left promptly, taking his share of the netherite with him.

Rajah watched him go. "That's not how it's supposed to work. He was meant to get down on one knee and swear eternal fealty to me. Maybe even become blood brothers. Slice open our palms and clasp hands in a manly fashion."

Where did he get these ideas from? "Not likely given how you are at the sight of blood. Your own especially."

"True allies share the bond of blood. Everyone knows that."

"Fine," said Faith. "Get a knife out. I'm ready whenever you are."

Rajah looked at her, bemused. "Between equals. Sir Tyrus is a noble. What don't you understand?"

"Enough, both of you." Pal hefted his rucksack. "We did it. Not Tyrus. Not his Bravos. Us. We got into the bastion and we got the treasure. That's what I understand."

Rajah shifted from foot to foot, casting an awkward glance from her to Pal and back. "Er . . . yes. Well done, Pal. And you, Faith. I . . . couldn't have done it without you."

Thanks from Rajah? Now, that was progress, wasn't it?

Her first proper quest. She'd survived. Now that it was over, the shock hit her hard. So many close calls. Any one of them could have turned to disaster. Now she was scared, but not back then, not when they'd been battling the ghast, the magma cubes, or the piglins. Why not? She'd been thrilled. Everything had felt so much sharper, so much more vivid. It had all mattered. She'd spent her life in the doldrums, on a still, stagnant sea. She'd not known what it was to feel the wind blowing, the rise and fall of the waves. She hadn't known such joy as when they'd been creeping through the shadow-filled bastion. She had found her purpose. That was it. She knew what she wanted, in the very depths of her soul. All those stories she'd grown up with—this was so much better. This was real, this was her life.

Returning to town, there were no cheering crowds. Everyone went about their own business, just like they did every day. Surely they noticed how she'd changed? The steeliness of her gaze, the confidence in her stride. The singed eyebrows? She'd expected them to stop, pause a moment, and perhaps tremble a little, awestruck by her transformation. Just a little. She'd changed, she felt like a different person, but the world wasn't remotely interested. She wanted to stop someone and tell them how amazing it had all been, how terrifying, how exciting. Recount the battles, blow by blow. "I thought it would be bigger deal."

Pal turned to her. "What?"

"Our adventure."

"That's what the bards are for. You just wait and see. A few coins in the right palm and you'll have the tale wrapped up in a fine bow. Boasting about your exploits always sounds better from another's lips."

It made sense, even if it sounded wrong. How would the bard know how it really felt, facing the ghast? Or that moment Pal's gunpowder blew down the wall? But she'd heard the storytellers when they'd passed through her village. They'd taken meals and a place to sleep in exchange for a song and tale. They'd found the words easily enough to weave enchantments over their audience, over her and the other young ones. Their words had been keys, unlocking magical realms of devilish danger, terrible monsters, and epic heroes. Now she realized she'd walked through that doorway to wonder and never really come back. She belonged in the magical realms, where the boundaries didn't exist, in those places off the map.

Ironic, really.

"Pure netherite," said the Mapmaker, turning the ingot in the sunlight. "Nothing else quite like it. More valuable than diamonds."

"Harder to find, too," said Rajah. "The Nether's not a nice place, even for heroes such as myself."

Myself? Had he really said that? Faith was about to remind him there'd been three of them on this quest, but Pal shook his head. It wasn't worth it. There was room for only one hero in the saga. They were the sidekicks. Not for the first time she wondered where Pal got the patience to stick with Rajah and his delusions of grandeur.

"And the map?" asked Rajah.

"This is all you have?" asked the Mapmaker.

Faith turned to Pal, arching an eyebrow. He put his finger to his lips. He wanted to keep his ingot secret. He wasn't convinced the map was authentic, so this way they would be left with more than a scrap of potentially useless parchment.

Rajah leaned across the table. "You should be grateful you have even that much. The other party you sent out came back empty-handed, didn't it?"

The Mapmaker smiled uneasily. "Other party?"

"The Bravos," said Faith. "What was the deal you made with them?"

"Oh, the Bravos! Ignore them. I knew it would be you who succeeded where so many others had failed."

"We saw their abandoned gear," said Pal. "The plain around the bastion was covered in them."

"No great reward comes without great risk," said the Mapmaker, tucking away the netherite. Then he laid out the map, gently unfurling it across the table. "As agreed. The path to Castle Redstone."

Rajah picked it up with the reverence usually given to religious texts. "The Great Swamp. Lightning Ridge. The city itself. It's just as Father told me. This is it, my chance to show everyone."

"We don't know how accurate it is. This road"—Pal drew his finger along a portion of the map. "How long is it? This isn't part of the realm I recognize."

"We're going beyond the boundaries of the realm. That's the point, surely? What sort of quest would we be on if others had already completed it? My father tried to find Castle Redstone for years. This was the one thing he failed to achieve. Think of how he'll greet me if I come back home having conquered the castle? He'll respect me, at last."

They were both trying to escape the past, but in different ways.

She wanted to get as far away as she could from everything her parents represented, the small-minded, isolated, and frightened view of the world, while Rajah was trying to be worthy, to match his dad's lofty status.

What about Pal? He had to have a reason to be here, more than just merely serving Rajah's every whim.

The Mapmaker bid them farewell. Rajah retreated to a table nearer the fireplace to pore over the map.

The tavern was crowded. Merchants mainly, people striking deals, swapping stories, laughing and feasting together. The air smelled rich with the meat roasting on the spit, and thick with the hubbub of all these people. Some adventurers across the room raised their glasses to them. Word of their journey to the Nether had spread. She wondered if Tyrus featured at all. She breathed it all in, absorbing the scene so it became part of her. She didn't even know the name of this place, but it felt more like home than the place she'd been born in. She couldn't even remember the color of her front door.

"What's next?" she asked.

Pal had taken out the netherite ingot and was inspecting it closely. "We'll resupply. Then tomorrow hit the road. So enjoy having a nice, warm bed tonight. We'll be sleeping in ditches or under the trees from now on."

"That's not so bad. It'll be fun sleeping under the stars."

"That all depends on what else is out there at night, doesn't it? We're going way off the beaten track, to lands unknown."

"To Castle Redstone, though! Think about it, Pal! We'll be the first to explore the place in who knows how long. You worry too much about what might go wrong instead of focusing on succeeding, on the prize."

"And what if you don't get the prize you've been chasing?"

"That doesn't matter. It's easier to walk along the rugged road with hope in your heart, rather than despair."

Pal laughed. "There's no stopping you, is there?"

"No. Nothing's going to stop me. It's all out there, Pal, and I want to see it. Back . . . in the place I grew up everyone seemed content with their lot. Maybe they were living the best lives they could lead, but they'd never looked. That's what got me. Go and see what's out there. Then decide."

"That's assuming there is a Castle Redstone. The map could be like the others, and we could be setting off on a fool's errand. And not for the first time."

"Then why do you go along?" she asked. "Whatever you think you owe Rajah, you've paid it back with interest. Go find a better life."

"Find a better life? I wouldn't even know where to start looking," he said. Faith couldn't miss the despair. "The journey's going to cost us, Faith. I don't mean just in coin, but also in what's here." He tapped his chest. "The Nether was in and out, over as quickly as it started. This is the long slog. There'll be nothing to show for it, not until the very end, if that. Most people don't have that sort of stamina. They want their treats right now. Instant rewards for an afternoon of effort."

"You think I'll give up?"

Pal stretched out and yawned. "We'll see."

CHAPTER 13

PAL WATCHED THE OTHERS at the shore. Rajah turned the map over and over, while Faith tried to match up the details on that rag to what lay before them, a series of islands nothing more than dots on the horizon. They needed to cross the sea, but this expanse was rarely traveled.

How long would he have to maintain this farce? When would Rajah realize he wasn't like his dad? That the life of an adventurer wasn't for him?

They'd been scammed, and it wasn't the first time. Rajah just had that look. Naïve and pompous, with a vastly inflated opinion of his own importance and abilities. A boy desperate to be a man. Those few tufts of hair on his chin fooled no one. All you needed to do was flatter him, Pal had seen it done over and over again, and Rajah would fall—tumble—for whatever sob story or money-making scheme was offered him. Pal had given up trying to persuade him out of it. Strange, wasn't it? You were always more likely to turn on your friends than disbelieve strangers selling stories that were always—always—too good to be true.

But weren't they in the same business, of selling stories? Was this about finding Castle Redstone, or about the tales that would spread afterward? Call it what you like, glory, reputation, legacy, it lasted longer than the gold.

Glory. What a joke.

Pal knew the price of it. Lord Maharajah's old manor had been a run-down, leaking, semi-derelict hovel by the end. He'd been too proud to do any other work; he was a famous adventurer and hero, not the sort to dirty his hands with labor. The farm had been abandoned, the fields grown wild while the old man had wandered his leaking halls boring anyone within earshot speaking of this battle or that triumph. Dust and cobwebs had gathered over the artifacts of that life. He couldn't escape his past, when he'd been *somebody*.

And Rajah wanted to be just like him. Why?

Why was fame the only thing that mattered nowadays? What did it matter if you were remembered after you were gone? The only things that appreciated statues were the silverfish.

Pal gave the three boats one last inspection. They weren't exactly pretty, and you needed to watch out for splinters when you sat down, but they would float and get them across the water to the next landmass. "They're ready."

The others returned from the water's edge. Rajah held the map up, comparing its markings with the islands out there. "We're looking for the Giant's Arch. Once we're through that, we're on our way."

"How long will it take?" Pal asked.

"I don't know," Rajah admitted. "But we've enough provisions for a few days and a fishing rod each. We'll be fine. Then after the arch we sail on to the mainland. From there we're on foot till we find Castle Redstone."

Pal shook his head. "Assuming the map's correct, or this is going to be the longest wild-goose chase ever."

Faith slapped his shoulder. "Let's get paddling."

There was nothing he could do to dissuade them. They loaded their gear in, and the three of them dragged their boats down into the water. The moment his caught the waves it became a living thing, bucking ferociously, riding the crests and swaying, trying to break free from them. Pal lost his footing and went under, coming up spluttering as Faith climbed aboard. She grabbed him and hauled him up. Once the boat was weighted down, it settled like a tamed horse. Faith nimbly swung herself up into hers.

"Sire?" Where was Rajah? Drowning at the start of the quest wasn't part of the plan. "Sire?"

But instead of succumbing to the waves Rajah was already settled his boat, making long smooth sweeps through the water. "Castle Redstone awaits!"

How about that?

Pal inspected the boat, making sure the planks remained tightly joined despite the hasty construction. Considering he'd never even seen the sea, he'd built a solid vessel. Sometimes you needed to just take satisfaction in a job well done. He'd made something good, something useful. Pal slid his hand along the planks, feeling the pressure of the water against the hull, listening to the waves lapping and the oars splashing with a steady, smooth rhythm.

One after the other, they joined up to be paddling side by side. A dolphin followed along before heading off to play elsewhere.

Rajah worked his oars with surprising grace. "Father found a shipwreck once. Had to wrestle a squid to get back to the surface."

"What was he after?" asked Faith. She always wanted more tales of the great Lord Maharajah.

"Some fabulous treasure," said Rajah. "I forget which."

The islands came into view soon after. They were uninhabited, but the remains of old, abandoned settlements still clung to the shore or along a clifftop. People could not stop themselves from building. But it was one island in particular they were searching for . . .

The Giant's Arch. It came into view slowly, as if rising out of the depths just for them, to mark the first part of the quest, to prove the accuracy of the map. It was a huge, tree-covered arch, draped with vines, lush emerald foliage, and swaths of flowers. Countless parrots nested within its crags; the sky echoed with their shrieks as they swarmed overhead. The current accelerated, catching hold of their small craft and carrying them under it.

Rajah sat cross-legged with the map spread over his thighs. "Through the arch, and head straight toward the setting sun."

Pal turned back to watch the beach, the realm, slowly retreat. Everything he'd known was back there. Not the best of lives, but the only one he knew. He didn't share the passion the other two had for lands unknown, for the thrill of planting one's foot upon a strange shore. Pal leaned against the hull of his boat, the boat he'd crafted himself. As the boat rocked rhythmically upon the sea, under the cloudy sky, he felt . . . satisfaction. You had to take joy in the little things.

"Pal, wake up." Faith shook his shoulder. "There's something down there."

Blinking away sleep, Pal sat up. The boats were bobbing under a clear night sky. The islands around them were black silhouettes upon the sparkling sea surface.

"Like what?" he asked.

Faith was peering over the side of her boat, then suddenly pointed. "There. See?"

"It's just a school of fish."

"Will you just look?"

Yawning, he leaned over and watched. The moonlight didn't penetrate far underwater, but he saw them, larger, single-eyed, swimming as a group around some indistinct underwater structure. Who'd build underwater? Then, suddenly, a flash of light burst from that single eye, illuminating the underwater ruin as brightly, and as briefly, as a lightning bolt.

"What's it made out of?" asked Faith. "I've never seen a stone that color before."

"Let's ask." Pal tapped his oar against Rajah's hull. "Wake up."

"Hmm?" Rajah had fallen asleep, hands still clasped around his fishing rod. He'd spent the journey fishing and had caught half a dozen brightly colored tropical fish. "Are we there yet?"

Pal gestured over the side of the boat. "What do you make of that? Someone's built a castle under the water."

"That?" said Rajah, dismissively. "It's an ocean monument. Hardly worth the effort of exploring, unless you like sponges. Looks pretty, though. Can't go wrong with prismarine. Father had the master bedroom decorated with it."

Faith was still gazing at it. "But who built it?"

Rajah shrugged. "Who cares?"

"What about those one-eyed things?" she continued, still fascinated by this new underwater world.

"I'd rather not find out." Pal took up his oars. Maybe these fish were territorial and wouldn't follow.

The fishing rod twitched. Rajah tightened his grip. "I've got something."

"Let it go, Rajah. We've got enough food to last awhile longer."

But Rajah wasn't listening. He was too busy struggling with the rod. "It's big! Here it comes!"

The creature burst from the water, flailing madly as Rajah hoisted it up in the air and brought it flopping down in the boat. It was big, a large round body with that weird single eye and a powerful thick tail section. Rajah reached for it, then yelled as spikes burst from its body. Then it swiveled in their direction.

"Get rid of it!" Pal yelled.

Rajah grabbed the discarded fishing rod and with a sharp twist flicked the creature across the water until it landed with a splash.

The water began to bubble as the other one-eyed monsters reacted to its thrashing by firing off their own beams. One buffeted against the boat, its spikes scraping the hull. Then the fish, sensing their target, began to converge on their little flotilla.

CHAPTER 14

LATER ON, HE'D LEARN they were called guardians. But right now in the middle of an uncharted sea, all Pal was interested in was flattening them with his paddle. They swam at his boat, spikes extended, trying to smash holes into the shivering planks. When they fired their crazy eye beams at it, the water would hiss and bubble, scorching the outside of the hull. Sooner or later they'd smash Pal's little boat apart. It wasn't a question of *if*, just *when*. And the *when* was getting closer by the moment. He slapped a head that got close to the surface, any eye that might rise out of the water, before it unleashed its devastating beam. Rajah stood up in his boat, shouting warnings. "There at the front! Quick! Another to port!"

"Get out of there!" yelled Faith.

The other two were out of the frenzied school. The guardians had decided they wanted *him*.

The boat shook as another one of the creatures rammed straight into it. A plank cracked and water jetted through.

He wasn't going to make it.

Faith shouted as she waved off to the distance. "There! There's a shore! Row, Pal! Row!"

Pal searched around frantically. There, a black line upon the water. Land? How far? It was impossible to tell. "I'll never make it!"

Faith started slapping the water with her paddle, trying to attract the things. "Just start rowing!"

He got working. Deep, long sweeps even as the aquatic monsters chased and continued their attacks. Beams laced the darkness, one getting close enough to singe Pal's eyebrows.

"Row!" Rajah yelled.

The hull was leaking badly now, cracks appearing on all sides. One guardian trapped itself when its spikes got stuck in the wood. Rajah finished it off with a swipe.

"Row! Row! Row!"

Did the creatures sense their plan? They attacked with increased ferocity, determined to sink Pal's beautiful boat before they got to shore. The bottom few inches were filled with water already.

A guardian crashed into the oar, knocking it from his hands. Pal reached out into the water to grab it even as the fish dragged its spikes along the back of his hand, but he managed to flick the fish back before it unleashed its eye beam. The water bubbled and steamed as it splashed back in.

The boat shuddered as another smashed straight through the weakened hull. It wedged itself half in, half out, thrashing to wriggle free, its beam cutting a searing line across the wood. Pal slammed it again and again until it fell out, but now water surged through the hole. With the integrity compromised, all the other cracks suddenly ruptured. Pal cried as he swept his oar and . . .

It scraped along the bottom.

Faith beached her own boat and was splashing through the water toward him. "Out! Get out!"

A beam pierced the weakened wood, perforating the hull once and for all. Despite being soaked, the wood briefly caught alight. That was enough for him. Pal grabbed his gear and leapt out of the boat. The guardian consumed it in a frenzy, ripping the boat apart while the three of them rushed for the shore. Rajah grabbed him and hauled him the last few yards out of the waves. Then, only then, Pal collapsed to his knees.

Rajah squatted down beside him. "Pal? Are you hurt? Please tell me you're okay."

"I'm okay."

Rajah hugged him. The boy was stronger than he looked.

"I'm okay, sire."

Rajah broke apart suddenly. It must have been seawater in his eyes, surely not tears. "That's good. Of course you are."

The boat barely held its shape. Beams lanced up from the depths, burning deep, smoking grooves along what remained of the hull. Other fish continued ramming the wreckage, reducing each and every plank to splinters. Soon enough the only thing left of Pal's boat was the floating debris. The sea darkened as the fish stopped using their eye beams. They swam up and down the shoreline, as if still searching for victims, then gradually turned and with powerful, languid flicks returned to the deeper waters.

"Are you all right?" asked Faith.

"Fine. Just leave me here. I've had enough."

"On this beach? But we're *here*, Pal. We've crossed the Uncharted Sea, this must be the land of the old kingdoms. We've done it."

Slowly and with great reluctance, Pal got back up. "This is the old kingdoms? It looks no different from the realm."

Rajah waved the map in front of him. "We made it! This is just as the map described. See those hills? They're shown right here. Let's get going."

"Yes, sire," sighed Pal. "Whatever you say."

He pulled on his rucksack while Rajah went on ahead.

"He's left his rucksack," said Pal. He knew why. Carrying it was Pal's job. You couldn't have a noble lugging heavy equipment like some mule, could you? That was the job for peasants like him.

Not anymore.

Rajah frowned as he caught up with him. "Where's my rucksack?"

"Back on the beach, sire. Where you left it."

"But why didn't you bring it?" He looked genuinely confused.

"What am I to you, sire? Your nursemaid? Here to give you a cup of hot milk before tucking you in for the night?"

Rajah just stared at him.

He had no idea, at all. Pal was just there, not quite part of the scenery, but a constant presence that had been around to help Rajah along the path of glory, or whatever ambition he had. But Rajah's path was not his own. Now they were betting their lives on a treasure map, and Pal wanted his say to matter. He gestured to the rucksack in the sand. "It's right there."

Rajah collected it and rejoined them. "It's quite heavy."

"Yes, it is."

Then Rajah did the most unusual thing. He held out the map for all three of them to see. "There's a path here, following the river. What do you think?"

He was asking their opinion. Pal tried to work out the details better. "How about this? It's shorter."

"It is, but it goes through a swamp. It's easier to get lost."

Pal looked to Faith, but she wasn't offering an opinion one way or the other. Then Rajah nodded and rolled up the map. "We'll try your idea. We could always double back if things get difficult. Do you agree?"

Pal nodded. He wasn't used to making decisions, or being asked his opinion. It felt weird, like an extra weight was being added into his rucksack. But it was a burden worth carrying.

"The swamp, then," he said.

CHAPTER 15

NO ONE IN FAITH'S village had ever been more than five miles from their front door, yet here she was, in the old kingdoms. What would her parents think? Her friends? Would they be amazed, proud? Or would they just be bewildered? Wasn't home enough?

Maybe. Once the quest was over, once she'd seen all she wanted to see, Faith might turn back and head home. But at least she would have *seen* what the rest of the world had to offer. She'd have basked in its wonders and overcome its dangers.

So far Rajah's map had been true. And if it was true up to here, thought Faith, why not the rest? Castle Redstone was here.

They found a village and while the locals were friendly, their language was unintelligible. They traded for food and Rajah matched up some of the landmarks to his map. Pal remained unconvinced, complaining that the water had damaged the map and was that really a river marked or just stains? But every night he made sure they had a shelter, turning his hands and mind swiftly and efficiently to whatever the task was, so despite his constant grumbling, Faith had to admit Pal kept them going.

Rajah? He walked in a cloud of old stories.

"Did I tell you about the time Father fought off a whole army of illagers?"

"Maybe once. Was that when he—"

"He'd gotten separated from his party, been wandering alone throughout the entire night when he saw lights in the distance. He thought it was a friendly village so he marched straight in, shouting for a hot bath and a plate of mutton chops! Then the illagers, plus their evoker headman and his vindicator guards, came pouring out of their hovels. Father was surrounded, but he had Heartbreaker. The bards still sing of the battle even now."

"They'll have new songs soon enough," said Faith.

"I doubt it. Father's retired for a while."

"No, I mean tales about you." Then, as an afterthought, "And us. Probably as a footnote."

Rajah stopped dead in his tracks. "About me? I mean, us?"

How could someone with so much ego have so little confidence? Faith slapped his shoulder. "Who else made it to the old kingdoms?"

There were more tales, one for every mile along the winding dirt tracks, across fields of long grass, and through the scattered woods. They found abandoned constructions that defied categories: Were they statues, works of art, or were they dwellings? Now fallen into ruin, they were almost impossible to make any sense of, but Pal would explore each, climbing over the debris and rubble, trying to rebuild the original structure, even if only in his mind. "That's where it all starts," he said, tapping his forehead. "If you can imagine it, you can make it."

"That simple? Then why don't we all build grand palaces?"

Pal looked over at Rajah. "We do. Just not for ourselves. That's our misfortune. Most people never fulfill their dreams because they've been conned into fulfilling the dreams of others at the cost of their own. What's the most precious resource in all the world?"

It was a trick question, she was sure of it, but guessed anyway. "Netherite?"

"Time. You can always dig up more netherite, but time? When it's gone, it's gone forever."

Faith laughed. "You a philosopher now, Pal?"

"I'm not sure what I am, not anymore. I never had much of a plan for my life, and now I'm looking back and thinking how little I have to show for it. I don't mean the lack of statues, but something solid I can be proud of, say to people, 'Look, I did that.' Leave my mark on the world, even in a little way. What about you?"

Faith took a deep breath. The air smelled different here, or maybe it was just her imagination. The sunlight in the old kingdoms had a different hue than back home. Or maybe her view had changed. She didn't look at the same old things the same old way. "What do I want? No idea. I'm not sure I want anything much. Does there have to be a plan, a goal? Being here, on the road, with you guys is good enough for me. I'm not searching for anything 'better.' What I have is great."

"No burdens but your rucksack. I envy you, Faith. I spent my life worrying about everything, thinking doom was just around the corner. That nothing good, or worthwhile, lay ahead of me. Servants aren't expected to have hopes or dreams of their own. I suppose I should thank Rajah for getting me out of the manor.

I've spent too much of my life already with my head bowed, never enjoying the view."

"And Rajah? Think he gets homesick at all?"

Pal looked over toward him. "No. The atmosphere at the manor was more stifling, more soul-sucking, than a tomb. It was a place of memories, obsessed with the past. Rajah needed to get out, and if he knows what's good for him, he'll never go back."

"The only way is forward, eh?"

What path they'd been following faded away soon after. This was wild territory now. But it hadn't been, once. Though the forest was dark and immense, they still stumbled across signs of habitation. There were moss-covered hillocks that, at closer inspection, revealed themselves as dwellings. They found the remains of roads, the once perfectly fitting stones disheveled by vines and sprouting weeds.

And redstone.

He missed it the first time, because the color of the circuits had faded to earthy brown. They were so broken there was no way of making any sense of their original purpose. But it meant they were on the right track. Castle Redstone lay ahead of them.

And then what would they do when they found it?

"This is good, really good," said Faith as she finished off the remains of the stew they'd been cooking. "You've found your special talent, Rajah."

Pal had given up trying to get her to use his proper title, and strangely Rajah himself didn't seem to mind, much.

"It's all about finding the right ingredients. Flavor is everything. The meat's just the start of a meal," said Rajah. "Cook used to take me out to find the vegetables. It wasn't the only thing she brewed, though."

"Oh? What else?" asked Faith.

Rajah stirred the pot with a stick. "Potions. Cook had a great big book filled with recipes, and the shelves were stacked with all sorts of strange ingredients. Nether wart, of course, but also blaze powder, spider eyes, ghast tears—you name it and she had a bottle of it up there, all with a neat label. She started teaching me, but . . ." Rajah's face fell. ". . . but Father forbade it. He didn't want his son turning into a cook. That was servant's work. No offense, Pal."

Pal had stopped being offended at his status a long time ago. "You spent more time in the kitchen than you did training in the courtyard. It's a shame Cook left when she did."

They all did, sooner or later. Of all the servants, he was the only one to stay. Maybe servitude was too deep in his bones for him to be anything other than what he was.

"I was happy in the kitchen," said Rajah, quietly. He stood up. "There'll be some interesting roots growing around here. I'll go gather a few for tonight's meal."

Pal picked at his own bone, methodically stripping off every trace of meat. Faith was right, it did taste really good. Better than anything he could conjure up.

The bushes ahead shook. Rajah must have found the ingredients he'd been looking for. "We're over here, sire! Just past the—"

A wolf stepped out from the foliage. It faced Pal, shoulders quivering and haunches tense, its legs coiled and ready to launch itself straight at him.

"Er . . . good doggie." He swung his stick over to his left. "Go fetch."

The wolf growled and certainly didn't "go fetch."

"What are you waiting for?" he muttered from the side of his mouth. "Shoot it."

"Why? It's harmless. If you leave it alone, it'll leave you alone."

How could she be so dismissive? Didn't she see those teeth? Its claws? Pal lowered his hand toward his pickaxe dangling from his belt.

The wolf bared its teeth and tensed, ready to spring.

The bushes off to the side shook and he thought this was it, the whole pack would descend and tear them limb from limb, but instead of a pack of howling wolves out came Rajah, holding a handful of roots. "Look what I found! These are delicious! Pal, you light a fire and . . . what's going on?"

The wolf snarled, replying for all of them.

Rajah sighed. "What a cute little puppy! He reminds me of Shaggy. You remember Shaggy, don't you, Pal?"

Puppy? Cute? Sometimes Rajah's peculiar view of the world could be really irritating.

"Hit it with your axe, sire."

"I will not! And none of you should do anything to hurt it! Can't you see it just wants to be friends? Look, I'll show you."

He wasn't going . . . oh no. "Stop, Rajah!"

Rajah picked up a discarded bone and waved it toward the wolf. "Who wants a snack? You do, don't you? Yes, you do."

Rajah fumbled for his pickaxe but the wolf bounded from tussock to tussock toward the smiling Rajah. It leapt at him, springing high through the air, jaws wide open . . .

And snatched the bone right from his hand. It settled down beside the fire, chewing ferociously, tail wagging. Rajah laughed as he grabbed the beast's thick fur and shook the animal roughly. The wolf barked.

Faith chuckled. "Looks like you've lost your place as Rajah's BFF."

It definitely did. The wolf slobbered over Rajah, who play-fought with the big beast. He couldn't remember seeing Rajah that happy.

Faith put her hand on his shoulder. "Time to move on, Pal."

In more ways than one.

CHAPTER 16

"IS IT STILL FOLLOWING us?" asked Pal.

A bark and Rajah's laughter from somewhere behind confirmed his worst suspicions. They were stuck with the mangy wolf.

He had hoped the beast would have given up once they'd entered the swamp. Surely the stench of rotting vegetation would have discouraged it? Sadly, not at all. And the wolf wasn't at all bothered by the insects incessantly buzzing around its ears, unlike the rest of them.

Faith waded through the swamp water beside him. "He's not so bad. Didn't you ever have a pet?"

"Yeah. I suppose I did."

"There you go! What was he called?"

Pal glanced back. He could just make out the pair of them. "Rajah."

"Careful, Pal. That rebellious streak's going to get you in trouble."

As if they weren't in trouble enough. "How can a place stink in so many different ways? Look at this . . ." Pal drew his thumb down his sleeve, collecting a gooey, gluey splotch of green gunk. ". . . it's dripping from the trees. Is it poisonous?"

Faith glanced up from her emptying swamp water from her boots. "I wouldn't put it on your bread, that's for sure."

"Thanks for pointing out the totally obvious."

"Anytime," she replied.

Why was he doing this? Life wasn't some game to be wasted on fool's errands. He could be living a better, easier life. One without Rajah, the swamp, and all the dreary misery of trying to be a hero. A hero. He hated the word.

A baker. A blacksmith. Even a builder. What was wrong with being one of those? Everyone needed bread. Heroes, not so much.

"You ever wonder about that moment you took the wrong path? Don't you wish there was a way to start it all over again? Turn a handle or press a button and have another go? I've just realized that all this time, I thought I was practicing for the real event. Never thought this was it. I always thought that if I just got through this, the rest would be plain sailing."

"Like our last boat trip?" asked Faith. "When you were almost torn to pieces?"

"That's not the point I was making and you know it."

Faith shook her head. "My point is there's no plain sailing, Pal. You just need to enjoy the ups and the downs. Nothing bad lasts forever."

"It's not forever I'm worried about, it's the right now." He dragged himself over to a tussock and dropped his rucksack, then himself. He pulled off his boots and gave his toes a wiggle. That felt good. Where were they, anyway? Was this swamp even on the map? And if it was, every direction looked the same, murky and fetid. Gases floated upon the surface of the stagnant pools, moss and vines hung from the serpentine boughs, and the vegetation had a sickly look and even worse odor. Frogs croaked incessantly. What he'd thought hanging fruit turned out to be leather-winged bats. Unhappy at being woken, they'd surrounded them in a cloud of flapping black wings before flying off. Sure, they were harmless, but . . .

Then he stopped and looked around. "Where's Rajah gone?"

"Wasn't he with you?"

Oh no. He'd just turned his back for one moment. "Rajah! Where are you?"

Nothing but the frogs croaking from their lily pads. Pal waded back into the mire. "Rajah! Rajah!"

Finally Pal spotted him and waded toward Rajah and the wolf. "We should get going. There's drier land up ahead. We could camp—"

The wolf snarled before he was within arm's reach. The beast's eyes flashed at him, and the message was clear. *Back off.*

Rajah wagged his finger in front of the wolf's snout. "No. Don't be like that. Pal's a friend."

The wolf wasn't convinced, but it closed its mouth, leaving the threat of attack rumbling in the back of its throat. Then it barked and bounded off.

Phew. Got rid of the monstrous thing. Now they could focus on getting out of this hideous place.

"Where are you going?" asked Rajah. "We need to follow the wolf."

"But it looks drier over that way," said Pal, pointing to a patch of moss-covered dirt. "And since when did that mangy beast join our party?"

"Since now."

That was it. "We should vote on it."

Rajah laughed. "So how many votes do I get?"

"We all get one each."

Rajah stared at him as if he'd said the world was round. "That's the most ridiculous thing I've ever heard. I'm far more important than the both of you. I should get at least ten."

"But that means we'd always have to do what you say!"

Rajah nodded. "Well . . . obviously. I don't make the rules, Pal."

The wolf barked, waiting for them to come along.

He was cold, soaked through, tired, and hungry. But he wasn't going to win this argument. Rajah genuinely didn't understand how he felt. The guy's view of the world began and ended at the end of his nose. That was the problem with heroes: It was all about them. The rest? Just part of the scenery.

They camped under a twisted, dead tree. The stench of the swamp still surrounded them, clogging their nostrils and coating the backs of their throats with a vile taste—but they were dry. Pal warmed his boots and socks near the fire while Rajah prepared the food. That was a servant's job but Rajah had insisted on it, and Pal was more than happy to let him cook their evening stew. The wolf sat nearby, paws crossed, watching Rajah work while its tongue dangled expectantly from its slack jaws. But each time the beast caught Pal looking at it, it would snarl. Rajah found it amusing.

"Don't be jealous," said Faith. "You can't beat a wolf. They're just happiness wrapped up in fur."

"It's not that," he said. "At least not all of it. We're lost, Faith.

Sure, this is a good place to camp tonight, but what about tomorrow?"

Rajah chopped up the last of the meat. He tossed a chunk to the wolf who snatched it out of the air, then scraped the rest into the pot. He added some beetroot and the smell, Pal had to admit, made his mouth water.

Faith sat cross-legged, checking her arrows. "The swamp doesn't go on forever. We'll get out of it soon."

"We're going around in circles, Faith. According to the map we should already have crossed it."

"I wouldn't call that piece of rag exactly accurate, would you?"

There was no point getting her to agree with him. Then, did he want her to? He got up and grabbed his boots. "I'm going for an explore."

"Don't stray too far."

"I won't. I'll keep my eye on the campfire."

He wanted to get away. Not that they'd even notice.

As darkness fell the sounds from the swamp became louder, or just more noticeable. Frogs croaked, bats fluttered through the dark, and things rustled through the reeds and slithered along the wrinkled bark. The moon shone upon the dank water, and the mists weaving through the undergrowth glowed an ethereal white. Blue orchids blossomed among emerald leaves, their perfume sickly sweet.

He thought it was a tangle of trees at first, boughs and trunks all twisted together. But closer he realized it was a wooden hut, raised out of the swamp by stilts.

Pal climbed up and peered through the bars in the window. "Hello?"

"What are you doing?"

Pal spun at the voice behind him.

Faith arrived, with Rajah and the wolf not far behind. She gazed at the hut. "Someone doesn't like company."

Yeah. Why else pick this spot?

"Maybe we should go," she continued. "Leave them alone."

He didn't exactly disagree. "We're lost, Faith. This person will know how to get out of the swamp."

The wolf growled.

"What's wrong?" asked Rajah. "Come on."

But the wolf refused to move. It snapped its jaws as Rajah reached for it. "Now, that's just rude. I thought we were friends."

Pal knocked on the door. No one answered.

"Well?" he asked. "Shall we go in?"

Faith hesitated, then nodded.

The wolf barked again, then turned and ran into the darkness.

"Good riddance," muttered Pal. He pushed the door open.

A cauldron bubbled in the center of the room. Vegetables, mushrooms, roots, and a bowl filled with eyeballs lay spread out over a heavy table, its surface scarred by use. The pestle and mortar on the table contained bonemeal. Bottles lined a wall, some filled, others waiting. A crude bed, just a pile of smelly wool blankets upon a low, wooden frame, lay in the corner with a pair of boots tucked beneath.

"Not exactly cozy," said Pal.

"Maybe we should wait outside?" said Faith. "This place gives me the creeps."

He felt the same, but there was a stubborn part that just wanted things his way, just this once. "It'll be fine."

"I really think we should leave," said Faith. She reached down and brushed the debris aside and took hold of something. "Right now."

It was a skull.

The cackling came from the doorway. A figure stood there, blocking their escape. They were grotesque, dressed in filthy rags, their pointed hat bent like a chimney. Their skin was gray, scaled by disease, studded with warts. A black cat hissed at them from beside their heels.

Rajah performed an extravagant bow. "Apologies, friend. We were lost and attracted by your most delightful dwelling. Did you build it yourself?"

The person's eyes glowed beneath their heavy brow.

Rajah looked back at us. "I think they want their privacy. We should leave."

Sometimes Rajah did speak sense. Not often, but he was making a lot of sense right now. If the window had been bigger Pal would have been happy to go out through it. But there was only one exit, and this person was blocking it.

The moment Rajah stepped toward the stranger, they moved, grabbing something from deep within the folds of their cloak. Pal glimpsed a bottle, bluish mauve liquid sloshing within, just before they tossed it at them.

The glass shattered and the room was instantly filled with a stinking, green cloud. There was no escape. The fumes entered his nostrils and filled his brain, making thinking thick, slow, hard. Pal felt his body drift away from him. The person's cackles were the last thing he heard before collapsing onto the bare wooden floor.

CHAPTER 17

"I WONDER IF FATHER ever had days like these? Or was it just one triumph after another?" said Rajah.

"He failed plenty," said Pal, sitting in his cage with his knees up by his chin. "He just never told you those stories."

Rajah twisted around within his own cage. "How do you know them?"

"How else? Do you really think the servants don't talk among themselves? That we don't have our own lives?" Pal scowled. "Of course you don't. You don't think at all."

"I wish he'd told me. Things might have been different," said Rajah. "This is your fault, Pal. What was it you said? Oh, look. There's a nice old person, why don't we ask them? Nice people don't live in swamps."

"I know that now," muttered Pal. He was too weary, too uncomfortable to argue with Rajah. What was the point, anyway? Rajah's head was so full of himself, there was no room for any dissenting voices. "Maybe we can explain our situation?"

"They know our situation. They put us in it. Where are they, anyway?"

Faith swung her own cage around so it rocked closer to the window. "Out in the garden. I've a bad feeling about this."

"Yeah, I saw the size of the chopping board. Who do you think will be cooked first?"

"It's not going to happen." Faith tugged at her bars. "There has to be a way out of here."

"And that's because . . . ?"

Faith pressed her back against one set of bars and began pushing her boots against the set opposite. She heaved, but the bars remained stubbornly fixed. "My story doesn't end with me as a witch's Sunday lunch."

"That depends on who's writing it, you or the witch. Theirs is clearly a cookbook."

"Instead of just complaining, why don't you do something?"

"Like what?" asked Pal. "You tell me how we're going to get out of this and I'll do everything I can to help. But there's nothing, is there? We're caged up and the witch is going to put us in their big steaming cauldron."

"And you're fine with that? Seriously? You're just giving up?" snapped Faith. "After all we've been through together?"

"There's nothing I can do, Faith."

Faith turned to Rajah. "Tell him!"

Rajah put his head in his hands. "Do what she tells you to. She's in charge."

"So you've given up too, eh? What happened to Sir Rajah, fabled son of Lord Maharajah? What happened to following in Daddy's footsteps?"

Rajah rocked idly back and forth. "Daddy's footsteps led us here."

Pal shrugged. "This is useless."

Rajah looked over at him, a disdainful sneer curling under his wispy mustache. "That's just typical Pal. Ready to quit at the first opportunity. I really don't know why Father insisted you accompany me. All you've done is grumble and moan every step of the way. This was meant to be a great adventure."

"Instead it's been a great pain in the backside. And do you know why your dad insisted I come? Someone needed to look out for you!"

"Then you've done a terrible job!"

"Boys! Stop it! This isn't helping!" yelled Faith. "Don't any of you get it? You're breaking the first rule of adventuring!"

That made them both pause. What was she going on about? "What rule?" asked Pal.

"Never split the party," she said.

Pal laughed. "We're not split. We're all trapped here together."

Faith tapped her forehead. "It's a state of mind. We work together. That's the only way we'll get out of this."

"You've been listening to too many tales." In some ways she was more naïve than Rajah. Pal shifted back and forth. He was going to get hold of Rajah and slap some sense into him, like he should have ages ago. "How old were you before you could tie up your own pants?"

"Nobles don't dress themselves! Everyone knows that! If we did, then you'd be out of a job! Ever think about that?"

"Doing up your pants was not how I intended to spend my life!"

Rajah laughed. "It's all you're good for!"

How dare he? Pal slammed his back against the bars, building up more momentum. The chains rattled and creaked as he swung closer to Rajah's cage. If he could get his hands around the boy's scrawny neck just once, he'd die happy.

Rajah stared as he swung closer. "What do you think you're doing? Get away!"

The cages crashed into each other. They spun away from each other, Rajah yelling as he collided with the shelves, bounced off, and swung wildly over the steaming cauldron.

Pal gripped the bars to steady himself. If he couldn't throttle Rajah he'd bash him all over the room and rattle some sense into what little brains he had.

"Look at what you've done!" snapped Rajah. "Are you trying to set me alight?" He'd knocked over a row of bottles and containers when he'd crashed into the shelves, and Rajah had been splashed with dust that fizzed and spat sparks over him.

"Oh, I suppose you want me to get a brush and clean it off? Forget it. You do your own chores from now on."

"Wait a moment," said Rajah. He tasted some of the dust, wincing as it fizzed on his tongue. "It's blaze powder. Cook used it to brew a potion for Father before he went off on a quest."

"What sort of potion?" asked Pal.

Rajah looked back at the shelves. Then he checked his pockets. "Nether wart. I've still got some." He took the plant and crushed it between his palms, letting it drop into the cauldron as he swung over it, then brushing off the blaze powder as he swung back. The brew began to bubble and hiss as the ingredients reacted with one another.

"You'd better know what you're doing," said Faith.

"Why break a habit of a lifetime?" grumbled Pal.

"Does it matter if I don't? We need to try something." Rajah pointed at the cauldron. "Look. It's changing color."

It was, and it stank. The liquid turned a deep purple, and great bubbles frothed and burst upon its surface.

"It's poison," said Faith. "It smells absolutely revolting."

But Rajah shook his head. "This is how the whole manor used to smell once Cook was done. But Father would fill up his potion bottles, have them dangling from his belt as he rode off. And Father wasn't the sort to use poison."

"Too honorable?" asked Faith.

"Too worried about poisoning himself." Rajah sniffed deeply. "It's ready. Whatever it is."

Rajah lay as flat as he could on the bars and wriggled his hand through the gap, squirming his arm through so he could almost touch the cauldron. "I need a push. Pal?"

"On it."

He started rocking again, slowly back and forth, just enough to give Rajah a tiny nudge.

Faith gasped. "Guys, the witch is coming back. Whatever you're doing, you need to do it right now."

"Almost there," said Rajah, his fingers stretching to the ladle hooked over the rim of the cauldron.

The witch whistled a merry tune as they splashed their way back to the hut, happy from the deep, honest delight that they had three plump morsels ready for chopping. Pal's gaze kept returning to the massive cleaver stuck to the heavy oak table. The surface was scored by dozens upon dozens of scratches and wedge-shaped dents.

The back door creaked open . . .

"Come on, stretch," whispered Pal. He shifted back, then jolted forward. This was his last chance.

The cage swung and spun toward Rajah, who had slipped his

arm through the bars right up to his shoulder. He clenched his tongue between his teeth and stretched his fingers for the ladle.

Their cages struck, and Rajah's spun off. But just as he passed beyond the cauldron his fingertips hooked up the ladle. He dipped the end in the cauldron's brew, splashing it wildly and spilling most of the ladle's contents before he pulled his arm back through and poured the few dregs into his mouth. Rajah grimaced and coughed.

Oh no. Maybe it was poison after all.

The back door swung open and the witch stood there, arms full of vegetables. Then they saw Rajah—ladle in hand—shrieked and hurled the produce aside.

Then they were hurled across the hovel into a stack of cooking gear as Faith crashed her own cage into them. "Do, something, Rajah!"

"I . . . I feel . . ." He turned a purple hue, and burped thunderously. "That's better."

The witch disentangled themselves from the broken crockery, then reached into their tattered purple robes and whipped out a bottle filled with a noxious green smoke.

"Rajah!" Pal yelled.

Rajah, sitting on the bars, his back braced against one side, thrust out his legs, slamming both feet flat and hard against the opposite bars.

And the entire door flew off, the chains snapping and the hinges shearing in half. The cage door smashed through the window and landed way down the path.

But he wasn't finished. Rajah leapt out of his cage and hauled the cauldron up above his head as if it were no heavier than a bucket. "Dinnertime, you hideous old crone."

The witch managed a wide-eyed squeak as the cauldron flew at them. And then . . .

"Splat," said Pal.

Only their feet stuck out from under the massive iron pot. The contents covered the floor and most of one wall, filling the room with a steamy stench.

It didn't take Rajah long to rip the other two cage doors open, but it took longer for Pal to straighten up his spine after a whole day curled up. He felt something twinge. But it could have been a whole lot worse. "I thought we were dead."

Rajah put a fist straight through a wall. He stared at the hole and grinned. "I feel amazing."

"No wonder your dad was able to beat all those monsters if he was guzzling that down before every fight." Faith went over to the shelf of empty bottles. "Let's scoop some of it up before it all drains away."

Rajah, though, started collecting the various ingredients. "These were all in our old kitchen. Huge jars and pots just filled with all sorts of herbs and powders. I can remember Cook going through them, making me memorize the names. She used them to brew her potions. It seems so obvious now. Look at this." He lifted up a pot. "Nether wart. You need this as the basic ingredient for most potions. Cook had shelves of it."

Pal picked up a small, severed appendage. "And this? A rabbit's foot? For a Potion of Hopping?"

Rajah took it from him and shoved it in his pocket. "Close enough."

Faith shoved as many of the bottles into her rucksack as she could. "Don't you feel a little bad about stealing all this?"

"Defeat the mob, steal the treasure." Rajah sniffed a jar of reddish powder before adding that to his rucksack. "It's what heroes do."

Pal picked through the gear from the other unfortunates that had ended in the cauldron. The place was littered with debris, buried under blankets of dust and sheets of cobwebs. But it gave him the creeps. Some things were better left alone. They should—

Pal turned at the sound of iron scraping upon stone.

The cauldron moved.

The witch's feet twitched.

"Guys." He started backing away toward the door. "It's time to leave."

A hellish wail came out from under the cauldron, echoing in the big empty vessel. Clawlike fingers slid around its bulbous form, gripping it tightly. The feet scuttled side-to-side and the cauldron rose.

"Run!" yelled Rajah.

The witch shoved the cauldron aside as they stood up. They'd been pretty foul before, but now they'd taken hideous to a whole new level. Then, with the awful sound of bones grinding against one another, they lurched toward them, reaching out with black-nailed claws.

Even Faith retreated. She shot Pal a terrified glance, and then they both turned and fled.

And the witch followed, their hideous cries rising.

They stumbled back into the swamp, the last place Pal wanted to be, but it was the only way out. He was already knee-deep, wading through the sludge and slime as the witch's cries grew louder. This was the witch's domain, and they knew the quick ways through the mire. Despite their mangled body, they were gaining.

Pal slipped. A moment later he was under the brackish water, flailing as he sank deeper into the weeds. The more he kicked, the more they entangled his legs. It was murky darkness beyond his hands, and sounds were muffled except for his gurgling as air bubbles slipped from his lips. Then a hand clasped his wrist and tugged. The weeds tore free and, spluttering, Pal was dragged up onto a grassy tuft. Faith wiped the muck from his face. "Now's not the time for a mud bath."

A twig snapped behind them and through the thicket of twisted black branches the witch came, all ragged, bloody, and full of cruel purpose. The witch smiled; they had them now. They dipped into their tattered robes and pulled out a bottle. A noxious, oily black liquid splashed within.

"That doesn't look healthy," said Pal. "Now would be a good time to put an arrow through their heart."

"Would love to, but my bow's somewhere in that quagmire."

The witch flicked off the stopper with their ragged black thumbnail.

Faith tensed. "You jump left, I'll go right. They can't get us both."

"What if it's explosive?"

"Just once, Pal, just once try to be positive. Okay?"

Pal crouched. "I'll go left."

"Thank you."

But he didn't need to, in the end. Which happened really quickly. A gray mass pounced out of the surrounding mist. It snarled, the witch screamed. They dropped the potion and it spilled harmlessly into the swamp.

But what followed was anything but harmless. The wolf slammed into the witch and both sank under as the water stewed and churned. The wolf briefly raised its head, its muzzle stained by the swamp water but its fangs draped with strips of purple cloth. Then it snarled and snapped at the witch as they tried to surface. Both went under again.

The waters stilled, then rippled as a few bubbles popped upon the surface. The wolf paddled out, its fur drenched in the foul swamp water. It joined them and spat angrily. Then it shook, muzzle to tip of tail.

"Perhaps having a wolf isn't so bad after all," admitted Pal as he wiped the gunk off its face.

Faith picked the strands of cloth from its fangs. "Don't like the taste of witch, eh?"

The wolf wagged its tail as Rajah emerged from the mist.

"I've been looking everywhere . . . hello boy!"

Rajah dropped to his knees as the wolf slobbered all over his face.

Pal just did not get it. Rajah used to complain about getting a speck of dirt on his linen, and now he was happy bathing in wolf spittle.

All of them were filthy. All of them stank. All of them were hungry, tired, and, face it, still a little scared. They were in the middle of a swamp! Other mobs, worse than the witch and even more hungry, could be lurking in the mists or under the algae-stained water.

"Good boy. We should have listened to you. You tried to warn us." Rajah buried his head into the wolf's soggy fur. "Good boy."

Faith waded back out of the water with her bow, wiping off the worst of the sludge. She plucked the bowstring as if were a harp. "Sounds fine."

"How can you tell?"

"You know when something's been made properly." She sat down beside him with a squelch. "Now what?"

"Back to the witch's hovel and have a proper poke around. We could find something useful."

"Then you're going in there alone. Try not to get lost in the mists."

The fog surrounded them, thicker than before. Strange sounds roamed through air, muffled and distorted by the deformed flora. "I think we're already lost."

"Good Boy knows the way, don't you?" Rajah held the wolf by his furry jowls. It was clearly love.

"That's his name? Good Boy?"

"That's his name because that's what he is. Aren't you? You're a good boy, Good Boy."

Judging by the tail-wagging, the wolf seemed pretty happy with the moniker. Pal reached out to pat him, but the wolf snarled. "Er, okay."

Typical. How come everyone else got to pat him?

They waded back and forth into the water to gather their scattered gear but eventually they had found almost everything, even Rajah's stone axe. Good Boy ran excited circles, barking and leaping with eagerness.

Rajah snapped his fingers and Good Boy joined him immediately.

Pal watched him. "How do you do that? He's a wild animal."

Rajah peered into the fog, Good Boy at his heel. He looked down at the wolf. "Do you know how to get out of here?"

Good Boy wagged his tail.

"Go on then. We're right behind you."

And Good Boy dashed off, barking.

Pal adjusted his rucksack. Everything was sodden, but he didn't fancy staying here a moment longer than necessary. Still, following a wolf? "We're really trusting our lives to a mangy mutt?"

"You have a better plan?" asked Faith.

"I'm just pointing out the flaw in this one."

Faith ruffled his hair. "We've gotten this far, haven't we?"

Good Boy was back, standing on a fallen, rotting log, barking impatiently. Rajah joined him and beckoned them to catch up. "Come on then! We don't want to split the party!"

He looked back at the swamp. The shredded remains of the witch's hat floated upon the murky waters. Maybe following the wolf wasn't such a bad idea after all. He seemed to know what he was doing. Which made a pleasant change. His bark rippled through the fog.

Perhaps the worst was behind them. The rest had to be a lot easier. Yeah, good times lay ahead. It was the law of averages, wasn't it?

It was about time something good happened.

CHAPTER 18

"I DON'T LIKE THE look of those clouds," said Faith. They'd been getting darker over the whole day, and she could feel the electricity in the air. "Looks like a storm's brewing."

Pal pointed to a cluster of buildings in the distance. "We could spend the night there, maybe?"

It was better than being caught out in the open, that was for sure. She nodded and started along the track. A meal, something to drink, and a chance to sleep in a bed. That's all she wanted right now. It looked like a nice place; the warm glow from the windows promised some cheer and even a chance to clean up. They all stank of swamp. The rucksack straps dug into her shoulders. She just wanted to get it off.

"There's a signpost up ahead," said Rajah, squinting to read it. "Mahar Town. Anyone heard of it?"

Faith shook her head. "I never knew there were dwellings this far west. I thought the world stopped at the Ridge Mountains."

Flashes of lightning lit the horizon and a cold, damp wind

whipped at their clothes. They were damp through already, but the wind cut like ice. Thunder rumbled as they reached the outskirts of the town and saw their first person: a villager carrying a basket filled with carrots.

Faith smiled at them. "Hello. We're looking for a place to sleep. Some food? We can pay."

But the person looked blankly at her, and Faith didn't understand their language. Faith put her palms together and rested her head against them, the universal sign for sleep. "A bed?"

They merely shook their head and wandered off.

Rajah rested his hand on his axe. "We could just boot a door down and rest up. These villagers don't look like they'd put up a fight."

"That's not what we do, Rajah."

"Oh, right," he replied. "You'd have thought I'd know the rules about being a hero by now. So simple in theory, so hard in practice. My father—"

"Hey, guys. Come and look at this." Pal stood facing a statue in the village square. "Does it remind you of anyone, Rajah?"

Rajah gasped. "It's . . . it's Father."

Faith looked back toward the signpost. "Mahar Town? Maharajah Town?"

Lightning struck a patch of earth outside the village. It was almost overhead. The villagers just went about their business, oblivious to the storm.

Rajah drew his axe. "We need to find shelter, Faith. Let's kick that door down and at least keep out of the rain."

"I said that's not what we—"

"Hey! You three! There's a storm coming!"

A man stood at an open doorway, waving at them. "Come in here! Quickly!"

They dashed toward the doorway as they were pelted by rain. Another lightning strike knocked off a chimney. If they'd been any closer . . .

They barged through the doorway and the man slammed it shut behind them. "What are you doing out in a storm? Don't you know how dangerous it is?"

But the other two weren't listening. They stood in the man's house, staring. There was a suit of armor on a stand, a sword over the mantelpiece, and a fine crossbow with a quiver full of bolts by the door. But hanging over the fireplace was a painting of a turbaned warrior. One glance at him, and at Rajah, and the familial resemblance was obvious. Rajah pointed at it. "Where did you get that?"

The man picked up his crossbow and loaded it. "Never mind that, the storm's right overhead. We've tried to warn them, time and time again, but they just don't understand."

"Understand what?" asked Faith.

The man glanced at her. "You any good with that bow?"

"What's going on?"

"Just stand by the window and get ready to shoot."

"Shoot what?" But she went to the window and saw a villager, that same one she'd tried to speak to, casually walking across the square with their basket of carrots. "Hey! Hey! Get inside! Can't you see there's a—"

The lightning struck the square. The flash filled the house with a brilliant, stark light just as the thunderclap shook it to its foundations. The thunder was still ringing in her ears and light still flashing in her eyes when she heard the man shout.

Smoke drifted in the square. The basket lay there, burned to charcoal. The villager? Where was . . .

A figure moved through the swirling smoke.

The villager twitched and slowly looked around, then broke into a cruel, heartless cackle. Their eyes seemed to glow. Good Boy growled.

"Another witch?" said Rajah, holding Good Boy back from bolting to the door. "Is that how they're made?"

The man hefted his crossbow to his shoulder. "Don't just stand there gawking!" He then swung the door open and took careful aim.

Her vision was still blurred but Faith drew and shot. Other arrows flew from other windows and doorways. The witch screamed as one struck. They retreated into the smoke, hiding them from the deadly volleys.

The man grabbed his sword. "We've got to drive them out before they do any harm. The last one poisoned the well."

Good Boy barked loudly and Rajah let him go, running off after him, axe aloft. Others, armed with swords, tridents, and even plain pickaxes, burst from their homes, shouting and yelling.

The witch hissed as the townsfolk surrounded them. Faith didn't dare shoot in case she hit the wrong person. One townsperson got too close and was splashed by a noxious potion. The harmless villager was gone and this cackling, vicious hag was all that remained.

Poisonous fumes spread across the square. Townsfolk coughed and wheezed as they breathed in the noxious gas, but the odds were stacked against the witch and they started retreating. Good Boy chased them but Rajah whistled and the wolf returned, growling with frustration, but obedient to its master. Some others chased after the witch to the edge of the town, then left them to flee into the darkness beyond.

The man returned to the house. "We're safe till the next time."

The villagers were still out and about. Some of the people who'd fought the witch were trying to reason with them even as the thunder rumbled on, but clearly to no avail. They just didn't speak the same language. The villagers just nodded, smiled, then went about their business, only briefly pausing to look at the freshly burned patch of earth where the lightning had struck.

"What happens to the witch?" asked Faith.

The man shrugged. "End up down in the swamp most likely. There are a few of them down there. It's part of the reason we've ended up so isolated. The swamp's become a dangerous place." He then looked over at her and wrinkled his nose. "And judging by the stench that's where you've just come from."

"We had some witch trouble while we were down there. Could have gone worse than it did."

Rajah was back with Good Boy. He stood at the door, staring at the man with a puzzled expression. "Where did you get that painting?"

The man gazed at it smiling. "I painted it. It's in honor of the greatest man I've ever known."

"You knew Lord Maharajah?" asked Pal.

"Lord now? I shouldn't be surprised. Probably saved a princess from a dragon and got half the kingdom. Am I right?"

"If you mean married the local farmer's daughter and lives in a falling-apart run-down manor with too much damp, you're completely right. So . . . how did you know him?"

"I was his squire, years ago."

Rajah's mouth fell open. "Harry?"

The guy turned back around to face them. "Yeah, that's right. Do I know you?"

Rajah shook his head. "By the Creator, you're Harry."

Harry still gazed at them, his bewilderment deepening. "What's going on?"

"I'm Rajah! Little Rajah! Remember me? You used to carry me around on your back when I was little!"

"Little . . . Rajah?" Then Harry laughed. "Maharajah's little boy? Let's have a look at you, lad! I should have guessed the moment I saw you! You've turned out a hero, just like your dad!"

"Not exactly like him . . ."

"Harry?" interrupted Pal. "The Harry?"

Harry was at the door, dragging Rajah along with him. "Everyone! You won't believe who it is! This is Rajah! Maharajah's little boy! He's come back to help us! I told you he would!"

They gathered around him. They slapped his back, they cheered his name. They hoisted Rajah onto their shoulders and paraded him around the houses with Good Boy barking excitedly alongside. Soon they were chanting his name.

Pal watched from the doorway as the crowd trundled past with Rajah carried aloft. "How about that? Rajah's the hero he always wanted to be."

"They named the town after his dad. You remember Harry?"

"Before my time. Rajah always went on about him. He was fond of him, that's for sure. He called all the servants 'Harry' after that."

"It sounds a little sad," said Faith.

"Lord Maharajah wasn't exactly the warmest of parents. Always more interested in the next quest or running off to slaughter another mob. He was always palming Rajah off on one servant or another. I always wondered what happened to Harry. Assumed he'd gone off to do some adventuring of his own."

Faith gazed around the room. As well as the weapons, Harry

had a collection of trophies from a life of adventure. Was that an egg from the Ender Dragon? "So he did. Seems he was pretty good."

She saw the adoration in the townsfolk's eyes. The joy that someone had come to save them. And who better than the son of the founder of the town? Why hadn't Lord Maharajah come back here himself? Had Harry been waiting all this time?

They returned, Harry, Rajah, and Good Boy. They waved off the last of the townsfolk and then Rajah turned to them, flush with happiness. "They love me!"

Faith arched an eyebrow. "They love the name. Now's your moment to live up to it."

"Did you hear them cheering? This was what my father was always going on about. It's better than all the gold in the realm. This is why he did it. This is what glory is." Rajah turned to the door and the fading chants of his name. "Isn't it magnificent? Don't you feel like you're shining?"

Faith dragged her finger across his tunic. "You're covered in swamp sludge, Rajah."

"Shining from inside! You wouldn't understand! They see the true me! The one that's a real hero!"

"Whoa. That's all dandy, but we all played a part in getting here, you know."

"There's only room for one name in the title," said Rajah. "The epic of Sir Rajah. Sounds . . . epic."

"The story's not over yet," said Pal. "There's still Castle Redstone to find."

Harry looked up. "Castle Redstone? That's where you're headed?"

Rajah nodded. "You know where it is?"

"I know. But it's not a place I'd send the son of my mentor. It's a cursed place, Rajah. You go there, and you'll join all the other ghosts."

"We've come too far to turn back," said Rajah.

"Who said anything about turning back? Stay here. This is your dad's town. And we could always do with another hero to fight the witches."

The door opened again and a woman entered with a heavy iron sword resting upon her shoulder. "I've done a patrol. The witch is long gone."

Rajah stared at her. "Cook?"

The woman frowned as she looked at him. Then slowly she smiled. "Little Rajah? Is that you?"

Harry put his arm around her. "Jane came with me when we left your dad. One thing led to another . . ."

"The manor was never the same when you left," said Rajah to the woman. "You made the place a home for everyone who lived there."

Cook, Jane, put her hand on Rajah's shoulder. "Our home is yours. You know that. Stay as long as you want."

Harry walked to a cupboard and pulled out a pile of clothes and dumped them on the table. "We can't have the son of a great hero wandering around in those rags. Here, try these. Something among them will fit you. But first, why don't you get your servants to draw you a bath? There's a well outside."

"Servants?" snapped Faith. "We're not his—"

"Where's this well?" interrupted Pal.

"In the garden. There's a bucket there, too."

Pal turned to her. "Come on, fellow servant. We've got work to do."

Faith glanced over at Rajah. He should back them up, that

they were companions, not servants, but Rajah was gazing at the portrait of his dad, lost in reminiscences.

Off to the well they went. The moment they were out of sight of the front door Faith turned on Pal. "What was that all about? You should have told that Harry we are not Rajah's little helpers. After all we've been through!"

"What?" asked Pal, distracted.

"You're not even listening!"

"To you complaining? No." Pal wandered off toward the square.

"Where are you going?"

He wasn't listening at all. He got like that more and more. Something was on his mind, and it took up all the space between his ears. Only one way to find out. "Wait for me!"

"This is where the lightning struck the villager," said Pal. He knocked her abandoned basket, and it crumbled to ash.

"So?"

Pal drummed the pickaxe hanging from his belt. "I wonder what's down there."

"What do you mean? It's just bad luck. Nothing we can do about it except drive off the witches when they emerge. I'm just worried about Rajah. Did you see the way he acted with Harry? It was like he was . . . home."

"But Lord Maharajah's manor's on the far side of the country now. He's never been here."

"Home's not just walls and a roof, Pal." Faith touched her chest. "You need to feel it in here. You said Rajah was never really happy in the manor. The only good times were when he was in the kitchens with Cook and with Harry. Maharajah was never the father he wanted, or needed."

"The guy was hard on him, that's for sure. I think he only got more so as the years passed and his own adventuring days got further away. He knew he couldn't go out and do all the great quests anymore, so he wanted Rajah to do them for him. Rajah never had a choice." Pal looked around the town and pointed at the statue. "That's Lord Maharajah at his best. Young, strong, noble, made out of stone, and no trouble to anyone. Better than the original."

"And look how they treat Rajah. They're giving him all the attention he craves. They believe in him more than he believes in himself."

Pal nodded. "That's the trouble with having a famous dad. No matter what you do it'll never be good enough."

They brought back the bucket and warmed it over the furnace. Rajah washed first, of course, then Faith and finally Pal, and by the end of it the water was green. Changed and fed, they gathered around the fireplace. There was something about the glow of a hearth. A homey magic. It wasn't flashy, but it was powerful. Rajah gazed at the flames, relaxed. That brittle tension he always held himself in had melted away.

Harry looked over at him, smiling. "The way you charged that witch! It was like your dad was back in action!"

"You think so? Really?" Rajah's yearning was obvious.

"Listen, lad. I served alongside Maharajah for years. Went on a dozen quests to all corners of the realm and beyond. You've got the same courage, the same nobility. Now that you're here, we'll all sleep a lot easier in our beds."

Faith caught the worried look from Pal. "Because of the witches? Can't you handle them?"

Jane tossed another log on the fire. "You saw us fight one, and it was a close thing even then. But sometimes the storm's so bad that it hits a crowd and suddenly we've got a coven of witches right on our doorstep. That's when things get really bad. The villagers just don't understand. We've tried over and over again to get them to go seek cover when the storm comes, but they just nod, smile, and go about their business. We've given up trying to get them to change their ways, but we can't just leave them."

"Don't worry, Jane. I'll help. For as long as it takes." Rajah sat there, lost in the flames. "It's what my father would have done."

He was changing the plan? Maybe Rajah needed a little reminder why they were here in the first place. "What about Castle Redstone? What about our quest? Isn't that what your father would have done, too? We've come so far, Rajah. We can't give up now when we're so close."

Harry snorted. "Castle Redstone? Forget it. We've seen so many adventurers pass this way, and none of them came back. There's only death waiting there, Rajah."

Faith leaned closer. "But you must have some sort of idea of what lurks there?"

Despite the closeness to the fire, Harry shivered. "Some ancient evil that destroyed an entire kingdom. We went there, back when we were younger, more foolish. Explored the empty, silent city, but never approached the castle itself."

"Why not?"

Harry sat deeper into his chair, letting the shadows deepen in his craggy face. "The place was as desolate as any I'd ever visited. No animals, no sound but the wind whispering through the ruins. And yet you felt as if you were being watched—no, more than that, preyed upon. Something dark and evil lurked there, waiting for someone foolish enough to fall into its clutches. The ruins were also barren, as if nature, too, abhorred it. There were just these black roses. Patches of them growing among the crumbling buildings. I didn't dare pluck even one. I'd adventured long enough to be wary of beauty."

"You didn't get anything?" asked Rajah. "All that way, for nothing?"

"I got this." Harry stood up and collected a jar from the shelf and handed it over to Rajah. "Look for yourself."

Rajah pulled the stopper out and sprinkled some of the contents, a reddish powder, onto his palm. "Redstone dust."

"It's yours. Never found much use for it. You could say the same for questing. There are better, more fruitful ways of spending your life."

"Depends on whether or not you succeed, doesn't it?" said Faith.

He looked up sharply, meeting her eyes suddenly. Faith almost flinched, the power of his gaze was so fierce, so dangerous. She shouldn't be tricked by the plain furnishings and simple living. Harry cleared his throat, embarrassed she'd seen through his façade. "It's late. I'm off to bed. We've got plenty of work ahead of us."

"We're not staying, Harry. Sooner or later Rajah will remember why he came here in the first place."

Harry smiled at her. "Or maybe it's time for your little party to end?"

CHAPTER 19

THE STORM HIT TWO days later and it hit hard. Lightning struck three villagers, and the newly created witches rampaged through the village for half the night before they were defeated. Pal had to drag himself back to bed and was asleep before his head hit the pillow. His last, conscious memory was of Rajah, Harry, and Jane singing and recounting every moment of that night's battle.

He woke just as exhausted, but outside Rajah was already training with Harry. Sweaty, covered in dirt, Rajah had never looked happier. He still fought with his stone axe, but he was putting real power behind his blows, spending the rest of the day in the nearby woods chopping down trees. As time passed, he started on building his own house beside his old servants. Faith stalked the village every night, trying to persuade them to pack up and leave, but each night it just degenerated into an argument, and now she and Rajah were hardly talking to each other. Pal? He was just stuck in the middle, as usual.

"She just doesn't get it," said Rajah as the two of them carried more stacks of wood to the plot. The foundations had gone down quickly and now they were erecting the walls. It would be built in no time and when it was, what then?

Pal lined up the next row of logs. "Get what?"

"Faith's a wanderer. She's only interested in what's over the horizon, but the horizon always stays ahead. You'll never reach it. Is that how you want to spend your life? Yearning for something you can never have?"

"Are you sure we're talking about Faith?" Pal asked.

Rajah stacked another row of logs to the wall. "I don't know what you mean."

"How long have we been at this? Do you even remember when we left the manor? What's the one good thing that's come out of all our mistakes and misadventures?"

"I'm not an idiot, Pal." Rajah wiped his forehead, his gaze heading back toward the village. "Faith."

"She's one of us, sire. You know the Number One Rule of adventuring?"

"Never split the party."

"I'm not wanting her to leave," said Rajah. "What's wrong with this place? These people love us."

"They love *you*. That's no small thing, I get it. After the way . . . you know. The way things were at the manor."

The muscles in Rajah's neck stiffened. "My father was a great man."

"Just not a good parent. But you're your own man now, Rajah. You don't need to be constantly looking over your shoulder to see if your dad's watching you. Disapproving. You don't need to measure yourself against him. Now this . . ." Pal pointed to the statue. "You're still working under his gaze, even if it's made out of stone.

Harry and Jane are decent people, but they belong to another part of your life, the past. You're their little boy, their mascot, and a memento of another time. You've moved on, because of Faith. You can't stop now. You stop now and you'll stay stuck in your father's shadow."

"He's given up," muttered Faith during one of their quiet moments. "He's acting like a fool. They're talking about making a statue of him, right next to his dad! Can you believe that? What has Rajah done, by himself? Nothing. He'd be nowhere if it weren't for us. Now he acts like we don't even exist."

"But he's happy." Even as he said it, he knew that was the exact wrong thing to say to her.

"Typical. You always put him first, always have, always will. What's he got you doing now? Darning his socks?"

"Building the smithy. We could do with better weapons, maybe some armor. Those witches are always going to be a threat. There's work to be done, if you're interested in looking."

"Then you're happy staying here, forever?" She shook her head. "I'm not. Castle Redstone's out there. We can't give up now. This is why we came out here. Not to just beat up a bunch of witches."

"No one's giving up. It's just plans change, Faith." Then he faced her. "Tell me you're not going off there by yourself, after everything Harry said?"

"How do we know Harry wasn't lying, just to get Rajah to stay?"

Pal shook his head. He'd seen how Harry and Jane were with Rajah. "They're family to him. He's not going to abandon them, and I wouldn't ask him to."

"Then that's it? You've seen how Good Boy's found himself a spot at the fireplace? Am I going to be saying the same about you? Found a comfortable spot by the hearth?"

He'd been thinking a lot about that, too. Harry and Jane were tending to Rajah's every need now. Rajah didn't need him anymore. "Maybe it's time for me to move on, too."

Faith was stunned. "You . . . you mean that?"

"This isn't home for me, Faith. Frankly I won't be too upset leaving it, sooner rather than later."

"The two of us? Fair enough." Faith put her fists on her hips. "There has to be something we can do here. Why do they have to live up here anyway? We could get them to move the village to somewhere less lightning-prone."

Pal laughed. "They can't even persuade the villagers to stay indoors during a storm. What makes you think they'll get them to relocate? Never going to happen."

"Then the lightning's going to carry on striking their stupid heads and they'll be plagued with witches forever."

Pal stood by the window. The village was on top of the ridge, prime spot for lightning strikes. But if you couldn't move the village . . . "We could move the lightning."

Faith laughed. "What? You're going to find a way to blow the clouds away each time they float over here? Good luck with that."

"I've seen it done, once. You plant a rod in the ground that attracts the lightning to it. If we did that, just outside the village, no one would ever get hit. And no more witches."

Faith frowned at him. "Do you remember what this rod was made of?"

"Copper. We could put a few outside the village, one north, south, east, and west, so whichever way the storm came there'd be a rod ready and waiting. We'd just need to make sure it was far away enough that no villager just wandered past it."

Faith's smile became a grin. "When can you get started?"

"How about now?"

They dug. They dug over the next few days until they found the copper, enough of it for Pal's project. Rajah avoided them to begin with, but soon his curiosity got the better of him and he found an excuse to visit the smithy where Pal was preparing the lightning rods. Rajah picked one up. "Funny sort of weapon."

Pal glanced over at Rajah and the weapon on his belt. "What happened to your axe?"

Rajah held up the sword. "What do you think? A replacement for Heartbreaker?"

The diamond blade looked sharper than Maharajah's old weapon, and more robust. Certainly a weapon worthy of a hero. "Harry gave you this?"

"He insisted. The trouble is . . . I don't want it. I haven't earned it." He returned his attention to the copper rods. "So what is this?"

"A shield, in a way. We're going to plant these around the village. If all goes well the lightning will strike the rods, keeping the villagers safe."

"Really? You think it'll work?" asked Rajah.

"We're going to try," said Pal. "Then Faith and I are off."

Rajah dropped the copper. "What? You can't leave."

"You're happy here, sire. You don't need us." Pal straightened up from his work. "We'll stop by on the way back."

Rajah looked genuinely upset. "But what about Rule Number One? Never splitting the party?"

"Aren't Harry and Jane your party now? Harry's got you sword fighting during the day and Jane's got you brewing potions in the evenings. Aren't you happy?"

"Happy? Yes," Rajah chewed his lip, something Pal remembered him doing when he was a boy. Rajah was slipping into old habits, it seemed. "But not content. Does that make sense?"

Pal didn't get it. Rajah and Faith had been arguing over this all week, but now? "What do you want, sire?"

"For you to stop calling me that," snapped Rajah. "Everyone calls me that around here. I thought I'd love it but the truth of it is I'm sick of it. They all treat me like my father, while Harry treats me like . . . never mind."

"Like what?"

"A little boy. The one he used to carry on his shoulders. He doesn't see I've grown up. That I'm my own man now."

"Are you?" asked Pal. "And who's he? This man?"

Rajah kicked the ground. "Not the one Harry remembers. But Harry was used to getting his own way. That was why he had to go, in the end. Father made him leave, for the sake of the other servants. Harry could get . . . rough. Never with me, but that's because I was his 'little boy.'"

Pal nodded. He'd seen the flashes of anger in Harry's eyes when they disagreed with him. He kept it under control, but it was clear Harry wasn't used to having his authority challenged, especially by a servant.

Rajah looked up at him. "When are you going?"

"After the next storm. We need to make sure these rods do their job."

Rajah gestured over to the west. "There'll be a storm tonight."

So soon? He'd thought . . . "Then we'll be off tomorrow."

CHAPTER 20

"A STORM'S COMING," WARNED Harry. "You need to get inside."

"I've got a little while longer yet," said Pal.

Harry looked at the rod skeptically. "You really think it'll work?"

Pal tilted the rod up onto his shoulder. "We'll find out soon enough, won't we?"

He slid the rod along the ground until the end fell into the hole he'd dug. Then he raised it up at his end until about a quarter was in the hole and secure enough for it to stand upright. He needed to be quick: The storm was on its way, and one way or another they'd find out if this worked. He drove the rod end farther into the soil, then began filling in the hole, shoveling quickly even as the air rumbled with distant thunder. "This'll work. I know it will."

"You need to get back inside," said Harry. "It's not safe."

"It will be. Don't you see, Harry? This is a lightning rod."

Harry was dressed for trouble. His had his armor on and his helmet was newly polished. His crossbow rested in the crook of his arm. None of the gear was new, but it was well made and well used. Under the helmet his eyes reflected the gathering storm clouds. "This is just foolishness. Your time would be better spent at the smithy, making weapons for us."

"I've got plans for that, too," said Pal. "I've been experimenting."

Harry laughed. "You've a busy brain, lad. I can see why Rajah thinks so highly of you."

"He's told you that?"

"You sound surprised. I know what it's like. I had your job once, when I served Maharajah. It's a strange relationship, if you think about it. It starts of as one thing, but after a few years on the road becomes something different. You've shared hardship, pain, and triumphs together. Seen things no one else has witnessed. Fought side by side until you don't know where one life ends and another begins. You're closer than any brother, any twin even, could ever be. That's how it is between you and Rajah."

Pal laughed. "It's nothing like that. I'm his servant, nothing more."

"You're all he has, Pal," snapped Harry. "He'll do anything for you."

Pal shoved in the next rod. "Are you sure we're talking about the same Rajah?"

Harry met his gaze. "I know him better than you. Rajah's not cut out for the adventurer's life. Anyone can see that. We can look after him here. Keep him safe. He's just—"

"A little boy?" interrupted Pal. "Is that why whenever you go out to fight witches, you're always near him, protecting him? I've seen how you make sure you're there to keep him out of real danger."

"And what's wrong with that? Rajah can't handle himself, not the way his father could. You've got too high expectations of him. You're just setting him up to fail and that's not fair on the boy."

Was Harry right? Pal had felt that, too, that Rajah was way out of his depth, but somehow it didn't seem right to treat Rajah like that. "Rajah wants to grow up. That means taking risks, pushing boundaries. That means facing uncertainty. This?" He gestured to the village and the brooding sky above. "This won't satisfy Rajah. Not in the long run."

Harry's gaze darkened. "Rocking the boat doesn't get you to the shore quicker, it only threatens to drown everyone."

"You think I'm rocking the boat?"

"You're a clever guy, no mistake. So tell me how this all works."

"Simple, really. The copper attracts the lightning. The lightning will hit the rod, there'll be a blast—that's why I've planted it just outside of the village—but then it discharges harmlessly into the ground. If we look after this, then the village will be kept safe from witches forever."

"And Rajah will be free to go off to Castle Redstone with you and Faith?"

Pal looked back at the village. "That's down to him, isn't it?"

Harry glared at him. "And let him get killed? I can't allow that."

"And that's not down to you, Harry. Rajah's his own man. Can't you see that?"

But he couldn't. Instead Harry grabbed one of the lightning rods and ripped it from the ground. "I am not going to let you drag Rajah to his death!"

Pal grabbed Harry's shoulder. "Put that back! The storm's almost upon us!"

Harry spun around suddenly, the rod in his hand. It struck Pal hard on the side of his head and there was a moment of dizziness as the world spun around and around, the ground rushed up toward him, and he fell, fell into darkness . . .

CHAPTER 21

FAITH SWUNG THE DOOR open. "What happened?"

Harry crossed the room and dropped Pal onto the bed. "He was attacked. A mob was roaming the edge of the woods. I was . . . just too late."

"I knew I should have gone with him," said Faith. "How is he? He's not . . ."

Jane sat on the bed, checking him. "He's breathing. But that's a bad injury."

"Is there anything you can do?" Faith asked.

The thunderclouds burst overhead and the room filled with the glare of a lightning bolt.

"The storm's almost upon us," said Harry. "We need to get out there. Rajah, are you ready?"

"I can't leave Pal. Faith, get my rucksack."

Harry stopped him. "There's nothing you can do for him. We need you, Rajah. The lightning's almost upon us."

"Pal is my friend," said Rajah. "You know my father would have done the same."

"Food. That's what he needs," said Jane. "That and rest."

Another, louder thunderclap burst overhead.

Harry held out Rajah's axe. "Here. We need you outside."

But Rajah shook his head. "Not until I know Pal's okay."

"He's just a servant! You can leave—"

"I'll go." Faith grabbed the axe. Harry resisted for a moment, glancing over at Rajah, but Rajah was busy checking the powders and potions he'd gathered from the witch's hovel. Eventually, reluctantly, Harry let go. "Fine. But stick close to me."

The wind howled through the village and yet the locals still went about their chores, oblivious to the churning black clouds overhead. The air crackled with power, and tiles rattled upon the roofs. This was going to be a bad one.

Faith swapped the axe from one hand to the other unable to find a comfortable grip. This weapon wasn't made for her. She wished she'd brought her bow, but there was no turning back; she didn't want Harry to think she was afraid or couldn't keep up. She knew he saw her as a threat, or a handicap, to Rajah's success. She needed to prove she deserved her place.

The rain hit hard and cold, stinging her bare cheeks and blurring her vision. Lightning illuminated the world for an eyeblink, revealing the dark landscape in stark, cold light. The storm was rolling in from the east, where Pal had gone to plant his last lightning rod. She'd done two herself, but they protected the village only from the north and west.

"We need to check the outskirts of the village," she shouted over the wind.

Harry had his sword drawn and gripped tightly in his fist. He nodded. "Lead the way."

"Where did you find Pal?"

He pointed toward the wood.

That didn't make sense. What was Pal doing way over there? No matter, that lightning was getting close. A dozen or so villagers milled around the market. If the lightning hit that, then they'd be overrun by fresh, crazed witches. They needed to check the eastern lightning rod.

They waded against the wind, dragging one foot after the other. The trees swayed and creaked, and Faith had to cover her eyes from the grit thrown through the air.

Another lightning flash revealed the fallen rod. The air around them was charged with static. They needed the rod standing before the storm was overhead. She dropped her axe to lift the fallen rod. "Help me!"

"It's too late!" Harry pointed back to the village. "We need to get back!"

Dirt and gravel lay scattered around the rod. The hole nearby was littered with loose soil and the bottom of the rod itself encrusted with dirt. She ran her hand along the metal. What were these dents? Someone had hacked at the rod to get it out of the ground. A mob wouldn't do that.

She didn't even know why she turned, and as she turned she grasped the haft of the axe, swinging it in the same instant. She couldn't have heard him, not over the howling wind and the thunder, but she felt a sudden chill, and that's what made her act, that's what saved her.

The impact of the sword upon the axe drove her onto the ground. She rolled aside as, using both hands on the hilt, Harry swung the sword down, cleaving a trench through the dirt. The moment it took him to wrench it back out gave Faith the chance to get to her feet.

"Why are you doing this?" She backed away. If she got enough distance she could run for it. But Harry just circled around her, making sure he kept between her and the village.

"I'm trying to save him," sneered Harry. "You're leading him to his death."

"Rajah? He means that much to you?"

"He's like a son to me. And what are you planning? To go to Castle Redstone? He'll die there, like everyone else that's ever gone. I can't let that happen."

Harry launched a flurry, swinging his sword with blinding speed, jabbing at her when she least expected it, forcing her backward, farther away from the village, out of sight of anyone who might help. She mostly parried, but soon she was bleeding from half a dozen minor cuts. But she wasn't used to the axe, to this relentless assault. She could hardly hold her weapon while Harry seemed to be getting stronger. He knew there was only one way this would end. They both knew.

There was no point shouting; who would hear them over the roaring wind? She screamed as a lightning bolt struck the ground nearby, sprinkling them both with sparks.

Harry paused, allowing him to catch his breath, preparing for the final onslaught. "You should have left. I gave you so many chances. Just walked off in the middle of the night. Rajah wouldn't have come after you."

"Rule Number One. You never split the party."

Thunder and lightning burst overhead, so loud Faith felt it in her bones. She clutched the axe haft, dragging it before her, desperately hoping to ward off his attacks. But Harry took a wide leisurely sweep, knocking the axe out of her hands and sending it tumbling off. He jabbed at her and she stumbled over the rod, falling flat on her back.

Harry laughed. "How ironic. Who would have thought the rod would be the death of you?"

"Gloating? You think that's what Rajah would do?"

"He'll learn. You have to do whatever it takes to survive. That gets left out of the tales." Then he wrapped both hands around the sword hilt. He stood over her, framed by the storm behind him, and raised his weapon high over his head. "It's you or him."

The world flashed pure, devastating white to a deafening thunderclap. The lightning bolt struck the raised sword tip and blasted through Harry with such explosive force he was sent flying.

Faith lay there. Alive. Drenched, shivering in the cold rain, her ears ringing from the thunder, but alive.

But the storm raged, and she still had work to do. She dragged the rod back over to the hole and twisted it back into place. She packed the dirt around the base with the flat of her axe, now badly chipped by the sword blows, then stomped on it to make doubly sure. She stumbled away.

The lightning struck the rod. The metal glowed with heat, but remained firmly fixed. A second bolt struck it a few moments later, attracted away from the village by this lure of copper.

They'd done it.

In the distance the villagers went about their business, as oblivious as ever. Would they even notice these rods? Did they even care? Strange places bred strange folk.

Harry groaned.

So he was alive. She'd not expected that. For a moment she thought about leaving him there, a tempting target for a lightning bolt, but then went to collect him.

He did look . . . frazzled. Smoke rose from his singed leather armor, and he now had a scorched bald patch on the crown of his head. She wondered if any hair would grow back. She hoped not. "Come on, then. Let's get you to bed."

If he heard or understood, he gave no sign apart from another pitiful groan. He was alive, and she was glad, funnily enough. He was doing this for Rajah. And so was she.

Is there a better feeling than the start of a journey? Dew evaporated under the warming influence of the morning sun, last night's rainfall scented the air with freshness, and the loaf in her hand was warm from the oven.

"Leave that bandage alone," said Faith when she saw Pal trying to scratch his head.

"It itches worse than lice." But he did as she asked. "The guy tried to bash my brains out and we're just letting him get away with it?"

"He was struck by lightning. I don't think he got away with anything."

Pal's scowl didn't shift even as he joined her to bathe in the sunlight. "Hasn't stirred since you brought him back."

"And we'll be long gone before he does. All three of us." Faith patted his shoulder. "Thanks to you and your brain. I'm glad it's still sitting in that fragile shell of a skull."

Pal smiled broadly. "Not one witch last night. I told you those rods would work."

"And with Rajah gone there'll be no reason for Harry to tear them out. He and Jane can get on with their own lives."

Pal nudged her. "Here he comes."

Rajah stood at the doorway, hugging Jane. There were tears and he blew his nose loudly on his handkerchief before wandering over to them. "I wish I'd said a proper goodbye to Harry."

She and Pal exchanged brief looks. They'd agreed not to tell him what had really happened. What was the point of spoiling that one bit of happiness? "He's still not woken?" Faith asked. "Not said anything?"

"Nothing that makes any sense," replied Rajah, after a long pause. "Well done on those rods. They'll make life a lot easier for everyone."

"Got everything?" she asked.

He held up a leather-bound book. "Jane gave me this. Her recipe book."

Faith smacked her lips. "So it'll be five-course feasts every night from now on?"

"There's more in the book than just meals." Rajah slid his axe from his belt strap. "This took a battering last night. What happened?"

Faith met his gaze. Despite appearances, Rajah wasn't entirely stupid. Faith shrugged. "This and that."

"This and that left cracks all along it. One decent whack and the whole thing may shatter."

"Let me have a look," said Pal.

He inspected it closer, ran his thumb over the edge, and sucked his teeth. Then Pal walked across to a nearby tree and swung. The axe bit into the trunk, and the blade cracked in two. Pal nodded, apparently satisfied. He tossed the haft aside. "Let's go then."

Rajah stared at the half blade still sticking from the trunk, then at the oh-so-casual Pal. "But that was my only weapon!"

Pal pointed over to the smithy. "That is your weapon."

It stood, resting against the post. The edge glinted in the sunlight. The blade itself was polished, gleaming black. Rajah approached it, awestruck. He wrapped his hand around the hilt and lifted the black sword. "What metal is this? It's not iron."

"Netherite. It took a while to get the quantities right. Have a swing at the anvil."

Rajah looked horrified. Then, mouth fixed in a tight, grim line, he raised the sword over his head and swung.

The blade cleaved the anvil in two. The halves thudded down into the dirt.

"I don't deserve this," said Rajah, holding the blade in front of him. "It's too good for me. Even my father never had a weapon this marvelous."

It always came back to Maharajah, no matter what. It might have been better to test the sword on the statue, get rid of that looming presence once and for all. Faith would be glad never to see it again. "You're not the hero your father was . . ."

Rajah's eyes flickered with that familiar look of failure, of defeat. "Of course not."

". . . you'll be better."

There was nothing left to say. They put their boots upon the cobblestone path through the village, passing the square, and Faith did, briefly, glance at the statue. Maharajah just had his nose stuck up in the air, too full of his own self-importance to notice them go by. The villagers chatted in their strange tongue, smiling pleasantly at them, but otherwise just getting on with their lives. Faith had no doubt by the time they were beyond the village boundary they'd be entirely forgotten. If they were curious about the rods, they showed no sign.

Faith patted the map tucked into her tunic. She and Jane had talked late into the night while Raj snored and Harry groaned.

She'd marked out the missing details. They'd not spoken about why Faith looked so disheveled, nor the wounds, nor why Harry no longer had his sword, but when Faith had dropped him in his bed, Jane had merely nodded and said, "It would be best if you're gone before he wakes."

"All of us?"

Jane had nodded. "All of you."

Rajah hadn't taken much persuading. The rods worked; the villagers could go about their business in peace. There was no need for heroes anymore.

The gentle farmland gave way to rugged wilderness. They camped in sheltered spots where Pal would build secure hideouts while Rajah cooked and Faith kept watch. They were far from the realm, far from her old life. She pored over the map in the light of the campfire, trying to gauge how far they still had to go, how much of the detail was correct. They passed by abandoned buildings. They were a hodgepodge of designs and materials—experiments, is what Pal called them.

And they came across the first redstone device.

It was simple, a bridge across a river with a gap in the middle.

"It's like the sliding floor back at the bastion," said Pal after walking up to the edge. "The break's neat and mirrored on the other side. There's a similar redstone circuit to the one on the treasury door but this time there's a line running over there to that stack of stones."

Rajah peered over at them. "Maybe they just didn't get around to finishing it."

"No. It's too well designed. Let's look."

Pal's instincts paid off. They found the lever hidden under the vines. Pal spat onto his palms and pulled it.

"Nothing's happening," said Rajah. "We'll have to swim."

Pal put his finger against his lips. "Shhh."

Faith pointed at the river. "Something's happening."

The water frothed and surged. Then a gray slab rose from beneath the surface. Section by section the middle span of the bridge rose from the water to fill the gap.

"Pistons," said Pal. "It's on a timer, so we'd better get going."

They crossed and just in the nick of time. The bridge shuddered while Faith was still on it, and behind her the slabs began sinking. By the time she was across they were entirely submerged once more. "Why?" she asked.

"Why not?" said Pal. "But it's a sign we're getting nearer. This must have been a toll bridge once. A guard would have stood there, charging those wanting to go across."

Rajah shrugged. "A simple wooden gate across the bridge would have done just as well. Why make it so complicated?"

"Somehow I don't think we've seen anything yet," said Pal, contemplating the bridge. "Whoever designed this was merely learning their craft. A lever, a circuit, and a couple of pistons. All pretty basic, when you think about it."

Rajah looked at Pal with fresh interest. "Only to you."

And so it went on. The landscape was feral, once civilized and now returned to wilderness. They found sections of cobblestone roads and more scattered buildings, now inhabited only by the wind and echoes. They camped within them, but reluctantly. Pal inspected the redstone circuits, which grew more and more complex as they proceeded, but few of the mechanisms worked now. That didn't stop Pal from spending every spare moment trying to put them back together.

"Do you know what you're doing?" asked Faith as she watched as Pal shifted a slab, rearranging the redstone circuit.

They were in a large, sprawling half-built castle complex. Someone with a passion for towers but lack of enthusiasm for foundations had once built their grand design—which, she reckoned, had collapsed during the first windy day. Who had the time to just dabble like this? What sort of society had come before them, where builders could just raise then discard their projects, their dreams? "What a waste."

Pal shook his head. "You don't get better unless you try, and fail. Enjoy the journey, not just the destination."

Good Boy started baying at the moon.

Faith groaned. "How am I meant to enjoy that? I don't know how you and Rajah can sleep through it."

"He'll shut up, eventually. Here, give me a hand with this block."

Faith jumped off the wall to take hold of the corner of the stone cube. "What do you want done with it?"

"Turn it so the circuit faces the other way, then drop it into that hole. See?"

She did.

They had to jump on the block itself to squeeze it into its place in the floor. Faith looked up and down the corridor. "But this doesn't go anywhere."

"Exactly. Someone didn't think this through. Dead ends make me suspicious."

She approached the far wall. "You think there's something on the other side of this? Wouldn't it be easier with a pickaxe?"

Pal turned to Rajah. "That redstone dust Harry gave you. Do you still have it?"

Even as Rajah handed it over, Pal was getting to work. He found a stick and dipped it into the jar of dust, giving it a twist to make sure the end was properly coated. The stick flickered, the dust sizzling at the end until it suddenly flamed.

"Didn't know it could do that," said Rajah. "It's not that bright, is it?"

"That's not what I want it for," said Pal as he slotted it in at the end of the circuit. The flames flickered, and suddenly the redstone circuit lit up. It ran all the way to the blank end wall.

And a moment later the wall slid open. Lights within flared to life.

"How did you know?" she asked.

"The outside wall is longer than the corridor. I knew there was more to it."

"You actually paced it out?"

"No. I just knew. I guess all those years running back and forth in Maharajah's manor in the dark just gave me a knack of measuring spaces." He wedged a stone block into the gap. "Just in case the door only opens on one side."

They wiped aside the cobwebs and entered a small chamber. The light illuminated a duty weapon and armor on a display stand and, curled up in a corner, the skeletal remains of an adventurer. The light created deep shadows within its eye sockets. It had its arms wrapped around itself.

"What a pitiful end," said Faith, squatting down for a better look, trying to guess the story from the remains. An adventurer, no different from any of them. A broken sword hinted at an escape attempt, and she could picture how they'd slipped the blade between the blocks to try to lever it back open. She promised herself that this wasn't going to be her end. "Found anything interesting?"

"No."

The leather crumbled to the touch and the armor was orange with rust, none of it usable, but that wasn't the point, not to Pal. He'd deciphered the circuit. They scanned the room briefly, but then turned and left. Once Pal had removed the stone block the wall section slid back, leaving the remains in their quiet tomb. Faith collected the torch, and the redstone circuit dimmed.

Good Boy continued howling. He paced around the camp, uneasy, teeth bared at the darkness. Rajah stood at the edge of the range of the campfire's light, nervously gripping the hilt of his netherite sword. "Good Boy senses something."

Faith drew an arrow. "Which direction?"

"I can't tell. One moment he's snarling over toward those rocks, the next he's barking at the trees."

Pal raised his hand. "Listen."

Rajah whistled and Good Boy retreated to his side. One tap of the muzzle and the wolf fell silent, though his hackles stood stiffly over the back of his neck.

Pal dipped a branch into the flames and once it was alight stepped deeper into the darkness. What was that sound? It was coming from all directions. He turned—

It might have been someone, once. Now it was just rotten, decaying flesh with a strange half-life, not truly dead, not truly alive.

A zombie.

They stared at each other, then the zombie thrust its hands at Pal, ragged nails clawing for his throat. Pal jabbed the flaming torch into its face.

It didn't even flinch. It kept on clawing for him even as the head caught alight. As the flames grew they illuminated more of the ruins, and more zombies climbing over the broken walls and scattered rubble. Rajah released Good Boy and the wolf bounded across the stones and slammed into one, sending them both tumbling.

Pal swung his pick. They'd gotten behind him somehow, blocking his way back to the camp. One had an arrow deep in its eye but didn't seem hindered by it. He gave it a solid blow and down it went, for now.

"That way!" shouted Faith from on top of a wall, arrows flying. "Into the ruins! Quickly!"

"What?" He struck another hard, the shock traveling all the way up the pickaxe into his arm.

Faith kicked one of the zombies off the wall. "They can only come at us from one direction! Stay here and we'll be surrounded."

More were headed toward her, but Faith leapt from one wall to the other, twisting as she landed to launch another shower of arrows. She waited, aiming carefully, then turned and fled as they got too near. All the while funneling the undead mob toward the narrow gap within the ruins.

Pal ran up to Rajah. "Come on. Faith's got a plan."

"A plan? Faith?" Rajah swiped off another head, but he was sweating and the sword sagged. He couldn't keep this up for much longer.

"There are too many, Rajah. We can't win."

"Hurry up, both of you!" yelled Faith.

Rajah grinned, despite everything. How could he be . . . enjoying this? "Well, you heard her."

They ran. Rajah whistled for Good Boy and joined Faith in a break in the wall. Easy to defend, plenty of rubble to hide behind, only one way for the mob to come at them. But they couldn't stay here; eventually they'd be overrun.

The zombies' macabre groans could almost be language. Did some faint spark of their living selves still exist, trapped within the rotten, worm-eaten flesh? What were they trying to say? Some dreadful secret from beyond the grave?

Nah. There was nothing there but a mindless hunger and a deep, uncontrollable hatred for life. Pal swung his pick at the nearest. "I could do with some help over here!"

Rajah whistled and Good Boy raised his head from the remains of the creature he'd just torn to shreds, then bolted over to Pal, barreling through the mob clustering around him. Rajah hacked his way toward him, sheering off limbs and heads, bisecting torsos and slicing through legs with effortless ease. That netherite blade was sharper than he'd imagined. Faith vaulted over a pile of rubble and then the three were back-to-back-to-back even as more of the undead crawled out of the darkness.

"I've not got many arrows left," said Faith even as she shot one through the forehead of a monster. It stumbled on a few steps before Rajah lopped its head off. "We need to find a safe haven. The zombies aren't active during the day."

Faith snapped her fingers. "The secret room. They won't be able to get in there."

Rajah shook his head. "And with the door shut we won't be able to get out."

"We'll find a way, won't we, Pal?" she asked.

"And if we don't?" Pal replied.

Another wave of zombies came shambling out of the night. "It's better than staying here!" she yelled. "Rajah! Clear the way!"

Rajah led, slicing through the crowd with Pal and Faith in his wake. The zombies were slow but tough. Faith shot her last arrow as the zombie was almost on her, and Pal bashed at it with his pickaxe, but more zombies came on, strengthened by the encroaching darkness. He turned: There was one in front of him. He turned again and again. All he saw was their dull-eyed, hellish faces getting closer. Rajah had hacked his way too far ahead of him. He couldn't turn back now without getting mobbed himself.

This was defeat, the final one. He'd fought and fought but sometimes it just wasn't enough. That didn't mean he was just going to curl up and die. Pal took a two-handed grip on his pick-axe, his eyes filled with rage, filled with defiance. "Come on, then!"

A hand landed on his shoulder and he spun, pickaxe raised ready to strike . . . until he saw Faith. "We're waiting for you, Pal."

"You shouldn't have come back, there are too many."

"Remember Rule Number One?" She was already climbing up the wall. "Follow me."

He didn't need to be told twice.

Over the rubble, over the broken remains of the castle they went, Faith beside him, watching for danger. He was exhausted, beyond exhausted, but she remained steadfast, guiding him along until he saw Rajah waving his gore-stained netherite sword. Good Boy barked at the sight of them.

Faith pushed him down the corridor. "This is down to you."

The groans of the zombies echoed from all directions. Good Boy snapped and snarled, desperate to launch himself into the heaving undead mass, but Rajah held him back. "Not wanting to rush you, Pal . . ."

Pal scrabbled to the secret door. The circuit ran straight into it. He slammed the torch down upon the circuit.

It should work. It worked last time, didn't it?

The truth was, he just wasn't sure, not about redstone. The lengths of the circuits, how to extend them, what power they transmitted, how many ways there were to do the same thing, and how many ways to get it wrong. Each time he tried, it was as if he was discovering it from scratch. What were its limits?

The circuit lit up and the door began to grind open. Faith helped it by shoving it with her shoulder; Pal stumbled in after. Good Boy was next, then Rajah, hacking off the closest pair of arms. The zombies were still reaching for them as the slab shut, crushing the zombie that had managed to get within arm's reach. The eyes of the monsters flared a hateful red, then the slab slammed shut and a few bones tumbled in. Pal stamped on them till they were dust, just to be sure.

Good Boy circled the small chamber, snarling at the old skeleton.

"He's no danger," Rajah told the beast. "We're safe."

"For now," said Pal. He still couldn't believe they'd made it.

"For now is good enough," Faith replied. "Might as well make ourselves comfortable. We're not going anywhere for a while."

He looked over at Faith as she arranged some rags to make a mat to sit on. He was shaking, yet she was acting as if she was just doing the housekeeping. She caught his gaze and winked.

They sat there, Good Boy curled up beside Rajah, and listened. They listened to the nails scratching at the stone, and the desperate, husky groans of the walking dead things, for the rest of the long, dark night.

CHAPTER 22

SUNLIGHT SLIPPED THROUGH THE cracks in the ancient walls. The air warmed under the light of a new day. Pal stirred at the sound of distant birdsong. Rajah sat by the door, his sword, blade bare, across his knees. "They've gone."

"You sure?" He didn't want to open up and find a horde of zombies sitting there, silently waiting.

Rajah nodded. "The smell's gone."

He was right. The putrid stench no longer contaminated the air. It was musty but no longer rotten.

They opened up the door and crept back out. There was no sign of last night's battle. Those zombies they'd destroyed had vanished, reduced to dust by the sunlight and carried away by the morning breeze.

In the distance lay the wall, the last feature upon Rajah's map. Beyond lay Castle Redstone. They could be there by tonight.

The others knew it, too. So did, somehow, Good Boy. He led the way, setting a pace quicker than they'd kept before.

The ruins were increasingly grand, increasingly elaborate. It was to be expected the closer they got to the heart of the old kingdom. This was where, a long time ago, the grandees had built their palaces and temples. The roads, though broken and uneven, were wider, as if the tributaries of the towns and villages on the outskirts had gathered to feed the river leading to the capital. Rail tracks ran alongside with their own branches heading off to the outskirts of the ancient kingdom. Idle minecarts still awaited filling. Pal tried to imagine what it must have been like in its heyday, the minecarts filled with animals, people, and the produce feeding the city, and the manufactured items being exported out. But while the buildings remained, the rest had merely disappeared. When they'd abandoned this place, they'd taken everything with them.

There were no signs of destruction by war—no scorched stones or blackened shells. Those buildings that had crumbled had done so through the weary work of the weather. Rain, ice, sun, and wind had destroyed these homes. Seeds had blown in through open windows and the trees had grown up through the roofs, their serpentine branches winding through windows and out of doorways.

But that great trunk road came to a sudden dead end. Right at the foot of the wall.

"It's a plateau," said Pal. "The city must be up there."

Rajah walked along the cliff face. "But the road just ends right here. Why?"

Faith tapped the rock with her boot. "It's not a wall. It's a door. Once it would have stood wide open, swallowing all the people coming to visit Castle Redstone."

Now that he was up close, Pal saw there was a logic to the door.

It comprised a series of square frames, each set within the other, getting smaller and smaller to end with four blocks in the middle.

The symmetry was the clue. He could imagine the hidden mechanisms pulling the blocks apart, each frame sliding into the next until they'd all retreated into the largest, leaving a wide, square opening. Simple and elegant.

"But how do we activate it?" he asked himself, gazing at the elaborate redstone patterns spreading out in all directions. "It's a puzzle. The circuit's all jumbled. We need to arrange it in the right sequence and then the path will open. But if we get it wrong"—Pal gazed up at the sheer cliff—"I guess something bad will happen."

"No surprise there," said Rajah, absently scratching Good Boy between the ears, much to the wolf's delight. "What about climbing? How high can it be?"

"High enough. And I don't want to get caught dangling off a cliff when the sun goes down."

Faith followed his gaze upward. "You think zombies can climb?"

"There's worse than zombies. We're off the map now. Whatever happened here, it was bad. And you see those cobwebs? Those cave openings? The cliff's infested."

She shivered. "Spiders? Ugh."

"We solve the puzzle. It's that simple."

Rajah frowned. "It looks the very opposite of simple. There's no sense to the pattern. What was it even meant to be?"

Pal had no idea. But the sun was already lower than he'd like. The door was immense; what vast mechanisms had to be behind it to make it open? You could attack it with pickaxes for a hundred years and not make it through. The ancient builders had taken their duties seriously.

So, the circuit . . .

It was the size of a field and impossible to comprehend when you were standing in it. He needed to get higher. "Wait here."

"Where are you going?" asked Faith.

Pal pointed at a ledge above them. "There. I need to see the whole design, or lack of one."

Faith looked down at her steadily lengthening shadow. "Be quick."

Take it one handhold at a time. Don't worry about the height. Just the next nub or crack for your fingers and foot. And don't look down.

Up he went. The cliff was rougher than it first appeared, but you could make out more details when your nose was a few inches from the surface. He cringed as he put his hands through cobwebs a couple of times, watching for the web makers that were lurking within the crevasses. The sun was at his back, illuminating the holes and tunnels, enough to catch a glimpse of hairy limbs, and reflecting upon bulbous red eyes. But the spiders seemed to prefer the darkness and kept away.

Pal reached the ledge and clambered up. He took a moment to shake the ache from his arms, then sat down to admire the view.

It was all out there. The road back. Past the ruins, through Mahar Town and the swamp, to the town, and back all the way along the mud track that would take him to the manor. Was Maharajah standing at the door right now, pipe in hand, gazing to the east, wandering about them? Whether they were having an adventure? Could he imagine how far they'd come? It seemed impossible at the beginning, and yet here they were. Almost. There was just the matter of opening these gates.

The circuit had to be a hundred blocks wide and the same

long. So many pieces, none seeming to match with any other. How was he meant to make sense of this? But there had to be a pattern, a combination that worked.

How would he have done it?

It looked complicated, but surely it was just about opening a couple of doors? Judging by the tracks, they slid, rather than turning on hinges. So they were powered by pistons. No circuit ran more than fifteen blocks without needing a repeater.

The circuit was broken up by other materials. Obsidian blocks, cobblestone, chunks of granite, all obscuring the original design. These needed to go. If they went, then only the circuit was left.

The sun touched the horizon. The distant hills fell into shadows.

"Guys! You've got to destroy any section of the pattern that doesn't have redstone on it! Quickly!"

The spiders crept to the cave mouths but he needed to stay up here to see the pattern. One spider scuttled to the ledge, and Pal backed away as much as he could. But the cliff wall was suddenly alive with the creatures.

Faith cupped her hands to her mouth. "We don't have time! We need to climb!"

"Just do as I say!" He threatened a spider with his pickaxe as it crept to the mouth of its nook. But there were more lurking in their dens, waiting for the sun to go down.

Faith and Rajah got on with it. They smashed away the blocks they didn't need, and slowly the pattern emerged. The ancient builders had constructed it like a cross, the circuits spreading out—left, right, up, and down—from the center. Exactly how the door would open.

He turned to the sound of rattling. A spider, the size of a horse, appeared at the mouth of one of the larger caves, but sitting upon it was a skeleton. It stirred as the light faded, its eyes beginning to glow with un-life. And it wasn't the only one. All over the cliff wall more of these uncanny riders emerged, raised from their slumber by the onset of night.

No wonder no one came this way.

The skeletons wore the remnants of armor, long rusted and covered in cobwebs. Their bows looked brittle, but as Pal ducked under the first flying arrow, it was clear they functioned perfectly. The spider began scuttling along the sheer cliff face toward him while its rider drew another arrow. There was no way to dodge it on this narrow ledge.

The arrow pierced the spider through its head. It died instantly, losing hold of the wall. It and its skeletal rider fell.

Faith, far below, nocked another arrow.

"How are we doing?" he yelled as another giant spider emerged from its hole, skeleton rider rattling its bones as it steered its mount toward Pal.

"Almost done!" Rajah yelled back. "Just hold on!"

Easier said than done. Instead of waiting to get perforated by arrows, Pal charged forward, swinging his pickaxe wildly. The skeleton tried to maneuver out of the way but too late. The pickaxe came swinging down, shattering the skeleton's brittle skull, and cracking the haft of the pickaxe. With no time to worry, Pal swung again, driving the tip of his weapon into the spider's side. The thing hissed and thrashed, but Pal gave it a shove and over the ledge it went.

"Ready when you are!" shouted Faith.

They'd removed the unnecessary blocks. The pattern was there. It just needed the gaps filled, linking the disparate sections into a single whole.

Pal fixed the design into his memory, then grabbed a dangling rope of spider string and swung off the ledge as more spiders converged on it. He shimmied down to the ground, the spiders sliding effortlessly on their own threads.

Faith and Rajah set to work. They smashed the nearest spiders and waved their torches at the others to drive them back.

Pal took out his supply of redstone dust and started laying it out. Did he have enough? Would the sections open separately, or all together? Was he even right? This was a circuit far larger than any he'd previously seen.

The sun vanished and it was night. The cliff was suddenly infested by spiders and their skeletal mounts.

Like a cross: As long as he kept that design in his mind he knew what he was doing. There was no time to doubt. This worked or it was all over.

The last of the dust went on.

Faith slammed her redstone torch at the center of the cross design.

And nothing happened.

CHAPTER 23

"NOT ENTIRELY UNEXPECTED," SAID Faith, wearily. Those spiders were worse than the zombies. They were still wary, the flames keeping them at bay, for now.

"It should work," said Pal, fighting the despair slowly filling his guts. "One of the circuits must be faulty."

Rajah hacked off the legs of one of the spiders, letting Good Boy finish it off. Faith had to admit the pair made a great team: Good Boy always knew exactly what Rajah seemed to want, and was more than happy to oblige.

"Can you get it working?" Faith took another step back from the spiders. They covered the ground, spreading in all directions.

Pal raced across the pattern, rearranging sections, turning them around, sliding them from place to place. "It's not a cross . . ."

What was he talking about? Faith kicked a nearby spider, sending it flipping over the encroaching horde.

Why did it always get like this? Just once, wouldn't it be great if the plan went smoothly? No hiccups, no last-minute panics, no sea of spiders or groaning zombie horde? *You wanted adventure, didn't you?*

Arrows spent, she thwacked another eight-legged horror with her bow. Rajah smashed one of the skeleton riders and tossed her its quiver. The moment she caught it she was shooting.

"It's not a cross . . ." Pal laughed as he pushed another block of circuit across the ground, dropping it into a new position. ". . . it's a star."

The cliff rumbled. Rocks tumbled as they were shaken loose, crushing not a few spiders on their descent. The ground shifted under her feet, and the spiders began to panic.

The gates opened. They slid into the cliff, all sections moving seamlessly together.

"Run!" yelled Pal.

She didn't need to be told twice. The spiders blocking her way? She jumped over them, jumped on them, ran over their carapace torsos like they were stepping-stones. Arrows hissed past. One skeleton rider scuttled toward her but then vanished under a blur of gray fur. Good Boy snapped his jaws over the thing's skull and ripped it off. The headless body did a rattling dance before collapsing into a heap.

They dashed through the gates. Faith grabbed an arrow and turned, ready for the horde of spiders to surge after them.

That didn't happen. They stopped at the edge of the now open cliff face. The skeleton riders paced back and forth, their own arrows nocked and bows half drawn, but didn't attack.

The walls rumbled and the five door sections slid back together.

Lantern light blossomed around them, revealing a vast, long

hall. There was an enormous pattern upon one wall, and a row of tracks beside a platform. A trio of carts sat upon the rails.

Faith stared at the pattern. There was no symmetry to it at all, just lines crisscrossing one another with symbols marked along them. "It's a map."

"A map of the city." Pal pointed to the single glowing block of powered redstone at the heart of the map. "Castle Redstone?"

Good Boy sniffed the rails and Rajah sniffed the cart. They were merging into a single personality shared by two separate bodies. She wasn't sure if she found it charming or a little bit freaky. Rajah tapped the front vehicle. "Who wants to ride at the front?"

"What do you reckon?" Faith asked.

Pal frowned as he gazed at the map. "I don't like how there are gaps. This map's damaged badly. If this is us"—he pointed at the star design—"and the powered block is where we want to be, then we've got to pass along this line, but some details have worn away or been purposely destroyed."

"But the alternative is us walking and getting lost. I don't know about you, but I don't fancy wandering around a mysterious cave complex forever."

"I'm just presenting the situation, good and bad. But it does look a long way on foot," Pal conceded. "Have you ever taken a cart ride?"

"At a fair, once. It wasn't that exciting." She climbed in the front, and Rajah went in the middle with Good Boy on his lap.

Pal inspected the map one last time, then pressed the central block in.

The carts began rolling. "Come on, Pal! We're off!"

The carts sped up. Pal ran alongside until he managed to get his fingertips on the rearmost cart and drag himself in. The carts continued to accelerate as they entered a tunnel. The lights were left behind and they were speeding in darkness. Good Boy's howls echoed back and forth through the long tunnel.

The carts rattled along the tracks, speeding until each turn and swing had them hanging on the edges. But soon the tracks steadied and ran straight, the wind whistling past.

Faith, at the front, noticed it first. She pointed ahead. "What's that?"

Pal groaned. "More bad news."

The rickety carts were heading to a chasm.

It had all being going so well up till now. Pal started looking for a brake mechanism. "That's what the map meant. This was blanked out because it was being repaired."

"Repaired?" asked Rajah. "Something's broken?"

Faith nodded. "Yeah. The bridge."

CHAPTER 24

"BAIL!" YELLED FAITH. SHE grabbed the edge of the cart and swung herself out. She hit the ground hard and rolled as best she could, which wasn't very good. She cut her palms on the loose stone, whacked the back of her head on the ground, and tore skin off her knees, but she, eventually and painfully, came to a halt. She waited for her head to stop spinning before she opened her eyes. When she did she saw Rajah standing over her, offering his hand. "Let me help you up."

"You're not hurt? How?"

"I've fallen off enough horses to have learned how to land. I'll teach you, if you want."

He helped her up. Faith gathered up her spilled arrows and shoved them back into her quiver. She joined Pal at the edge of the chasm. The rails had come to a sudden halt, and the cart was nowhere to be seen. There was only darkness in the depths.

"There's always something," she said.

Pal nodded. "There always is."

"How are we gonna get across?" Faith asked. "Could you build a bridge? There's plenty of stone here for you to work with."

"Work with what? My pickaxe broke fighting those spiders. We'd be a long time digging it up by hand."

"Or we could swim," said Rajah.

"That's lava, Rajah," said Faith.

Rajah rummaged around in his rucksack and drew out one of his potion bottles. "This will protect us. Enough to get across. It's one of Cook's old recipes, so I know it'll work."

"A Potion of Fire Resistance?" she asked. "How many have you got?"

He rummaged deeper, and out came three more bottles.

Pal smiled at the young man. "I don't know what we'd do without you, Rajah."

Faith took the bottle and held it up. "You think the brew's potent enough? That's quite a gap to cross."

"Honestly?" Rajah frowned. "I don't know. I haven't actually tested it, but I followed Cook's recipe exactly."

Trusting Pal's constructions was one thing, but a magic potion? There weren't any spares for them to test with a little dip; one bottle each and that was it. "Who first?"

"Me," said Rajah. "If a cook doesn't have faith in his own meals, then he's no cook."

She still wasn't used to this version of Rajah, the one who took risks for others. Had she changed as much? She felt the same, but perhaps you did, inside.

Rajah pulled off the cork and swallowed it in one gulp. He licked his lips and turned toward the gap. "It'll work. Trust me."

Trust him? She wanted to, but it wasn't easy. "Good luck."

He ran. Good Boy chased after him, barking excitedly, wondering what this game was but happy to play along with his master. Then Good Boy faltered as he got near the edge, and the bark became a warning as he watched his master dive off.

He disappeared under the lava in a gout of flame.

"Rajah!" yelled Faith. How could she have let him do in? She should have stopped him! She searched the surface of the lava, knowing she might glimpse a burned skeleton at any moment or, worse, hear Rajah's screams as he was burned alive.

Rajah burst through the surface. "Come on in! The lava's lovely and warm!" He then paddled across the gap and climbed up onto the ledge on the opposite side. "What are you waiting for?"

Faith shook her head. One successful swim didn't mean all the potions were equal strength. They'd been brewed by Rajah, after all. She couldn't get rid of the fear that disaster was just around the corner. Something *had* to go wrong.

Good Boy jumped and barked, unable to comprehend how Rajah had gotten all the way across. He dashed back to them, hopping and yapping as Pal took his sip. "I don't feel any different."

"You saw what Rajah did. Why shouldn't you do the same?"

"He's younger and more foolhardy than me. Ah well. Here goes."

Pal didn't dive in. He climbed down to the edge of the lava, hesitating as he watched it bubble and hiss. Then he dipped his foot in.

Faith braced herself for his agonizing scream, but instead Pal just . . . laughed. He waded in, right to his chest. "It's amazing. It really works."

He swam across and Rajah helped pull him out, shaking off

the flames that clung to his feet. Then Pal turned around to her, wiped the sweat away. "There's nothing to it!"

"Your turn," said Faith. Good Boy ran around her, wagging his tail, beyond excited. She poured the potion into the cup of her hand. "Come on then."

He lapped it up.

He wanted more. He jumped up against her, paws on her chest, snapping at the remaining bottle. "That's mine! Good Boy! Get down!"

But Good Boy wasn't listening. He jumped up, startled at the sudden height, and crashed against Faith. The bottle flew from her hand.

It hit the ground, spilling its precious liquid across the ground. Faith ran for it as the bottle rolled, tossing away more droplets. She grabbed it.

Good Boy whined miserably.

It was all but gone. Faith held it up, tilting it to gather the droplets clinging to the inside.

"Faith! How much is left!" yelled Pal.

"Enough!" she shouted back. "I'll be fine!"

There was only forward. There was no going back, not for her. She tipped the bottle upside down, catching every drop on her tongue. She'd expected her tongue to tingle, or feel something, but it barely had any taste. Was it enough?

"Come on, then." Faith patted her thigh, bringing Good Boy beside her. "Ready?"

Good Boy tensed, his eyes upon Rajah on the far side.

"Go!" Good Boy sprang off. Rajah called to him, arms outstretched, and Good Boy jumped as he reached the edge. There was a big splash and then he was paddling toward Rajah, who cheered him on. "Who's a good boy? Yes, you are! Come on, there's a good boy!"

See? Nothing to it.

She stood at the edge feeling the waves of heat rising from the churning lava. Surely her skin should be tingling with power?

But she couldn't stop. Not now, not ever.

On this side, all her past; on the other the future she would make for herself, beyond her humble beginnings, beyond the cloistered life of her village. Her toes touched the lip of the edge and she jumped, toward her future. Sometimes you just had to go for it.

And make a leap of faith.

CHAPTER 25

FAITH DIDN'T HAVE TIME to scream. The heat washed over her and then . . . then . . . she began kicking up toward the surface. The lava stirred around her, dragging on her limbs and pressing all around her, but the heat? She barely noticed it, just a light stinging sensation across her skin. Still, there was no need to linger. She kicked off and with big, strong strokes made her way across to the others. They cheered as Good Boy barked excitedly.

She was swimming across lava. Never in her wildest dreams had she though that even possible. If she could do this, then was anything impossible?

And as they hauled her out, Faith laughed.

Relief, yeah. She hadn't burned to death. But more than that. She was on the other side, with the people she cared about most in all the world. It was funny. The snooty Rajah and the dour, constantly grumbling Pal. But she wouldn't want it any other way. "Are you all right? You're sounding rather hysterical," said Rajah as he brushed the dirt off his tunic.

"You know how to brew, Rajah. Cook would be proud."

Rajah blushed but couldn't hide his grin. She doubted he'd have been more cheered if he'd been made king of the realm.

Upward. It was the only direction left. Along the tunnels, following the track, until they felt a breeze. Cool, but fresh.

It was a pinprick at first, a single speck of light in the darkness. They walked toward it, mesmerized as it slowly grew. The breeze was strong enough to ruffle her hair, and there was birdsong.

They emerged from the tunnel in the side of a hill. The track ran on, but there was no need to follow it; their destination was in sight. Buildings, ancient beyond the count of years, stood tall and proud, defiant against the ages that had come and gone. The pathways wound through them, between great statues and alongside gardens, now transformed into colorful forests. They'd reached the capital of the old kingdom. And there, rising like a crown at the heart of the city was a vast citadel, the center of it all.

Castle Redstone.

CHAPTER 26

"WHAT DO YOU THINK happened to everyone?" asked Rajah. "There're no signs of warfare. But why leave all this?"

Pal picked up a bowl. It was delicate, the work of a true artist, not the crude, coarse implement he was used to eating out of.

Faith raised her torch to admire the banners. The colors had long since faded but their intricate designs were just visible. Any lord or lady would be proud to have this hanging in their great hall. "They say the original rulers unleashed a terrible curse over the city. It couldn't be lifted, and so over time it spread to every part of the kingdom. The inhabitants were unable to combat it and after a final failed attempt, decided it was safer to abandon the city forever."

"And leave all their treasures behind," added Pal as he picked an emerald off the ground. He carried on, climbing over a fallen wall, and entered an area now overgrown with foliage. Trees and vines had broken through the walls, torn open the roof so sunlight fell upon a wild garden. The soft, cold breeze slipped through the cracks. Much of the garden was in gloom, the angle of the sun's rays brightening only a corner.

There were more of these peculiar black roses. These were in full bloom, their stalks guarded by thorns and the petals velvety. The perfume filled his nostrils, musky and soporific. His head swam as the scent penetrated deeper and he felt weighed down, burdened by . . . it all. The ground swayed and he reached out to call the others, but his arm seemed disconnected from him, and his vision blurred, Faith and Rajah seemed to stretch farther and farther away from him. They were leaving him.

And why shouldn't they? What use was he to them? He watched them talking to each other, sharing secrets he was not privy to. Faith entered another room and Rajah walked into the adjacent hall. Did he look back at Pal? Perhaps, but only to sneer.

The black roses surrounded him. He tried to brush them aside but winced as the thorns dug into the back of his hand. The perfume thickened and he swayed, slowly sinking to his knees. Why did no one help him?

Because you're not worth it.

He wasn't, was he? He'd been a fool to think he could be equal to the likes of Faith and Rajah. He'd been a burden from the very beginning. Even before that when he'd first been saved by Lord Maharajah. For years he'd hung around the manor, a constant shadow. Now he understood. Lord Maharajah had wanted to get rid of him. Rajah's loyalty had saved him, but now Rajah had Faith, someone better. It was time to let him go.

Let go. Just sink down into the dirt. Lie among the roses.

Pal touched the petals with his fingers. So soft. But cold. How could they be so cold? His heart sank, weighed down by a creeping weariness.

Yes, you're so tired, aren't you? You really can't continue anymore. This is as far as you'll go. Give up. You're useless, anyway. Leave the glory to the real heroes.

He'd thought they were his friends. He'd grown up with Rajah.

No, he'd grown up *behind* Rajah. There was a difference.

Why did he feel so exhausted? His limbs were as heavy as stone. He felt himself sinking, being smothered by the scent of the black roses. What dreams would come?

Something was wrong. Pal's vision began darkening. Everything around him became indistinct, faded. Or was he fading? He looked at his hands, and they were pale, lifeless. The bones visible beneath the thin skin.

"Help me," he whispered. He tried to shout but there was no breath in his lungs.

Pal lowered his face into the blooms surrounding him, breathing in their soporific scent. The petals brushed his cheeks, as if caressing him. Sleep here, sleep and never wake up. It wouldn't be so bad.

Yeah, not so bad. He was so tired.

Then something stung him. On one cheek, then the other.

Owww . . .

Fingers tightened around his biceps. They hurt! He just wanted to rest!

"Wake up, Pal!"

Who was that? His eyelids were so heavy, but he managed to push them open.

Rajah faced him, palm open, and slapped him.

"Wake up!"

Faith had him on his feet, his useless feet, and she slid under him so he didn't fall. "We need to get him out of the garden."

Why? It was so peaceful here. What were they doing? Pal tried to sink back into the dirt but with Rajah and Faith holding him up he could just squirm, forcing them to drag him along.

Then the perfume started fading and his head cleared. It wasn't quick, but Pal's vision returned, a strange brain fog lifted, and he felt the weight of weariness fade away. The others managed to haul him over the wall, away from the garden, but Pal planted his feet firmly on the stone floor. "I can stand."

Rajah raised his palm again, then lowered it. "Thought we lost you for a moment."

Pal shook his head. "What . . . happened?" Thinking wasn't easy. Each thought needed to be dragged out of the quagmire in his head.

"The black roses," said Rajah. "My father warned me about them. He wondered what happened to the original inhabitants and believed these roses are a symbol of their demise."

Pal turned back to the walled garden. "I was dreaming."

Rajah tightened his grip on his arm. "Only of despair, Pal. Such despair that you gave up. It's lucky we turned back and saw you."

He looked at Rajah, his oldest friend, and then Faith, his newest. "I thought you'd abandoned me. That's what the dream was. That I was all alone."

"Isn't that the greatest fear we all have?" said Faith.

Pal shook himself and looked upon his companions. They were there for him; he could depend upon that. And he was there for them. No one would have expected them to make it all this way, but they'd found strength in one another, and discovered talents and beliefs they didn't know they had. These black roses weren't going to take that away from him. But that still didn't answer the most important question. What had happened to the inhabitants?

They spread out across the silent city. They stayed within shouting distance, weapons ready, but found no danger. Everyone had simply vanished.

And yet . . .

The redstone circuits became more and more elaborate. Pal would sit upon a pedestal or atop a wall, pondering the designs, trying to fathom the mystery. He could spend a lifetime trying to untangle the wild and wonderful circuits, seeing if he might even bring it all back to life.

Wouldn't that be a thing?

Where to begin? In the heart of it all.

Castle Redstone.

The castle itself was a city within the city. The immense central keep of polished blackstone and basalt was surrounded by a sprawling, interconnected cluster of smaller fortifications, their marble roofs shining in the sunlight. Towers, some spiky nails of obsidian and others squat, tiered constructions of plain stone and cobblestone, rose from the corners of the main keep. Watchtowers lined sections of the ruined outer wall.

They approached the keep, gazing up and up at the colossal walls, trying to decipher the intricate patterns of inlaid lapis lazuli and sandstone.

"It's sealed shut," said Faith. "Not just the doors, but the windows have been filled in, too. They definitely didn't want anyone getting back in when they left."

Why had they been so determined to keep intruders out, when

they themselves had abandoned it? Had they thought they might come back one day?

Rajah tapped the iron door. "How do we get in?"

How indeed? The ancients had built Castle Redstone to last. The only way through was by playing by their rules. "They've purposely jumbled up the circuit. I need to work out what the correct arrangement is and then . . . voilà."

Rajah gazed at the foreboding entrance. "The doors should open in a majestic and awesome manner. I wish we had a bard to record all this."

Pal had rearranged the blocks, tested new circuits, but nothing had opened. Then he'd hit the door with the pickaxe, but that had only blunted his axe.

Pal tossed a piece of flint into the pool before the main entrance as he pondered what to try next. Lily pads drifted upon the murky water. Good Boy sniffed, his muzzle wrinkled with distaste.

It was a strange place to build such a feature, right in front of the main gate. To go in or out you'd need to go around it first, and that would be awkward in a vehicle—the gap between the pool and walls was small.

Why put it there, blocking the entrance?

Maybe that was the point . . .

The pool was long and rectangular, like a road. It led straight to the gate. He searched the floor until he found what he'd suspected. They'd been filled up with debris, but after scooping one out with his pickaxe he realized what they were: drains.

Too many to collect mere rainfall. They were to empty the pool.

He knocked a hole in the pool perimeter wall and watched the brackish water run out, following the subtle tilt of the floor slabs, and pour down the drain. He ran to the next section of wall and did the same. Four more times he broke away the old stone to let the water drain from the pool and expose . . .

A circuit.

This was it. "Rajah! Faith! Come here!"

They must have heard the excitement in his voice, because they came running.

The pool had drained out. The slabs beneath exposed a simple circuit leading from the gate to a rusty lever. The handle was covered in slime and rust. Pal hoped it wouldn't break, but he put both hands around it and eased it back.

The doors rumbled. Ancient pistons came back to life. Stone ground upon metal and, after an uncountable age, the iron doors to Castle Redstone groaned open.

CHAPTER 27

OBSIDIAN COLUMNS ROSE UP to towering heights to support a ceiling of glass, bringing a cold, fresh light into the vast entrance hall. Their footsteps echoed solemnly upon the intricately patterned flagstones of prismarine and glazed terra-cotta. There were the woven patterns of redstone circuitry spreading in all directions, repeaters installed with mathematical regularity and comparators opening doorways in methodical sequence, raising platforms, waking glowstone lights down the darkened corridors that branched off from here.

"The door opening must have activated the old circuits." Pal felt he was entering the belly of a waking beast as dust motes danced in its cavernous breath. "The castle been brought back to life after who knows how long?"

Rajah gazed at it in awe. "We did it. We actually did it."

Good Boy, so keen on exploring and sniffing the corners, wasn't being his usual self. He barely left Rajah's side, and his tail hung low. He growled at the shadows and whimpered at the strange, chill wind that whispered through the long-abandoned halls and corridors.

They *had* done it, and yet the mystery of the place remained. Why abandon this marvel? Pal looked back at the wide-open doorway. They could come and go as they pleased now, he'd out-witted the ancients, but he felt more like he'd betrayed them, somehow.

Why lock it up so tightly?

They ventured deeper, along the long quiet halls and passage-ways. Much of the place had fallen into ruin. Some circuits still performed their duties for the long-gone inhabitants. Tracks ran throughout the castle, more a walled city than a single structure. Great stone dragon statues guarded lavish, overgrown gardens. So much produce, enough to feed any town twice over, grew wild upon the scattered patches. There were fields of carrots, pump-kins, and mushrooms, and swaying forests of bamboo. They passed by crumbling chicken coops and animal pens.

And of course there were the black roses. They grew in the lonely places, thick carpets across halls, climbing up the towers, clinging to the walls, the sinister gloss of their petals both alluring and poisonous. Good Boy snarled as he got near them, sensing their danger better than they did.

"It's getting dark," said Rajah. "We should settle in for the night."

Dark already? Pal hadn't realized. "I'm not tired. I'll just do a little more searching."

"We have plenty of time for that tomorrow. And the day after. Day after that, too, if we need it." Rajah rummaged around in his rucksack and tossed a bone to Good Boy.

"First things first, eh?" said Pal.

Rajah looked up from rubbing Good Boy's fur. "What do you mean?"

"You're being pretty casual about all this. This is Castle Redstone, the castle at the end of the world. The one quest your father never completed. You should be celebrating."

"I am. So who wants mushroom soup?"

"Save some. I'm just going to have a little look around."

Faith slapped his shoulder. "Not too far, okay?"

Pal strolled along the lamplit corridors, trying to understand the design and absorb the thinking of the ancient builders. Eventually he found himself deep within the oldest part of the castle. Crumbling, squat, plain, and functional, it bore little resemblance to the extravagant construction that now dwarfed it. A chill wind moaned through the broken archways and derelict hall. A beam of moonlight pierced a gap in the roof, shining on the black roses. In this light they looked as if the petals were coated in blood.

A breath whispered against his back.

He wasn't alone.

Pal spun around. What ghost had risen from the cold stone? Had zombies followed them all the way here? He should never have left the others. He'd broken Rule Number One and was going to pay for it.

"Whoa," said Faith. "I'm on your side."

"Never do that again! You almost gave me a heart attack!"

"We were wondering where you'd gone." She turned her head over her shoulder. "Rajah! He's here!"

The other members of their merry band, Rajah and Good Boy, caught up with him. Rajah wiped his mouth clean. "The soup'll be cold by now."

"I wasn't lost. I would have found my way back. There's no way out anyway. The ancients locked this place up tight."

They approached a dark, shadow-swamped corner where for some reason the lamps weren't working. The circuit must have failed, not surprising since no one had been here for generations to maintain it. It was amazing so much still worked. Then he stopped dead.

Good Boy snarled, his hackles bristling and eyes bright with threat.

Rajah put one hand on the beast's shoulder. "He senses something. Something bad."

The bulky shadow ate the light. Instead of being dispelled by the glow of flickering flame, it became darker, an all-consuming void.

The shadow moved, and it was no trick of light. A great, dormant mass rose from its stone rest. It shook off dust and wrinkled rose petals that had fallen over it as it had slumbered. The thing hissed.

Good Boy started backing away, barking anxiously for them to follow.

Pal backed away as the eyes within its head filled his heart with a dread, almost paralyzing chill. Then another head swiveled around, and a third. The three-headed thing hovered just off the floor, turning slowly with a cloud of black motes, to look for whatever had woken it.

"What is it?" said Faith, nocking an arrow.

It was the ancients' great secret. The reason why their kingdom had ended with silence.

They'd not locked the doors to keep everyone out.

They'd abandoned their castle, their kingdom, to keep something *trapped*. To prevent it from terrorizing the world beyond Castle Redstone.

And Pal had flung the doors to freedom wide open.

He grabbed Faith by her shoulder. "We need to run."

"But what is it?" she asked.

Rajah knew; Pal could tell by the terror in his eyes. He'd been told about them all, the mobs that preyed upon people across the realm. Rajah started retreating backward alongside Good Boy, unable to take his gaze from the awful apparition that loomed over them. "The Wither."

CHAPTER 28

THEY RAN. NOT IN any particular direction, just away and as fast as they could. "A Wither?" asked Pal as they paused to catch their breath, get their bearings. "I thought your dad made them up!"

"Why would he do that?" said Rajah, checking his potions. Were any of them any use against the creature? Good Boy hid behind him, whimpering.

"It made a great spooky story. Something scary for the cold dark nights. Your dad was a great storyteller."

"All he did was talk about himself," said Rajah. "But . . . yes, they were good, and they were all real."

"So he must have fought a Wither then? How did he beat it?"

Rajah shook his head. "The thing killed his entire party. He barely made it home alive."

Faith swung around the corner. "I hear it, come on!"

The wall behind them erupted, filling the air with choking dust. The Wither loomed through the debris, firing explosive black wither skulls. Head ringing with the echoes of the explosions, Faith spun on her heels and loosed an arrow. At this range she couldn't miss. The monster barely flinched as the arrow struck. Good Boy darted in, snapping at the mob before dashing back, and Rajah hurled a potion bottle at it. The Wither shrieked, then erupted, hurling them back as the shock wave shattered the surroundings.

Faith shook herself, instinctively checking that her bow wasn't damaged. "What was that you hit it with?"

Rajah already had another in his hand. "Potion of Healing. Father said all that works in reverse when fighting undead."

"He wasn't wrong."

"Run!" Pal shouted as the black skulls flew.

They had to get back to the entrance. He had to close the doors, trap the thing inside. The ancients had imprisoned the creature, and it wanted to get out. If it did that, no one anywhere would be safe.

"This way!" Pal shouted, swinging around a corner with Good Boy at his heels. "Come on!"

Where were they? They'd been right behind him just moments ago!

He'd lost them!

The sounds of battle echoed throughout the castle. One moment it was as if they were in the next chamber, then it was as though Rajah and Faith were beyond the horizon. But wherever they were, they were in trouble. A series of dull explosions rocked the castle. Things were escalating rapidly.

Good Boy barked and dashed back and forth until Pal grabbed him. The beast was too worried about Rajah to snap at him, but Pal couldn't risk the wolf getting lost, too. "Stay with me. We'll find them together, okay?"

Good Boy whimpered but obeyed.

He had to get back and help! But even if he could work out where they were, what could he do? Pal checked his gear. There wasn't much more he could do with his mere pickaxe. And where were they?

He lit his torch and turned a full circle, slowly. The firelight reflected off tables, blocks of rusty iron, warped wood, and dusty stone, ores of different hues and textures. Under the dust were ancient tools and even a few bookshelves, their books and scrolls long turned to mulch. By the door was a lever. He pulled and the metal groaned as flakes of rust fell; then lights slowly came on, illuminating the chamber in uneven, amber patches.

Good Boy prowled through the huge chamber. Tables had been laid out at regular intervals and lines of material left abandoned, all in neat rows. He brushed his hands over the collection of ingots. Mostly iron under the dust, the surface spotted with rust but still solid, stone, diamond, emerald, obsidian, and of course raw redstone. There was more, but it would take him hours to check them all. This was a workshop with long rows of dusty crafting tables, tools and materials lying abandoned on them. Once this hall would have echoed with hammers and picks and chisels as the engineers and builders created their marvels. They would have loaded their creations into the carts and sent them hurtling along one network or another. Despite the fear gripping his heart Pal stood there, awestruck.

The books upon those shelves? He was sure they had been spellbooks. Why else would they have installed a library in here? He was sure if he wandered some more he'd find cauldrons and brewing equipment and shelves filled with bottles of ingredients. Given time, he could create anything here. Anything.

Given time.

Which he didn't have.

Pal rushed to the bookcases, tearing out books, one after another, but they crumbled in his hands. Not one remained whole enough for him to use. There were half-made swords, bits of armor, made of diamond and even netherite. All he needed was a few enchantments to make them deadly against the Wither, but there were none. He was going to have to find another way.

Come on, Pal. Everything you need is right here. Just come up with something!

Weapons? Even if he clad them all in the best armor and the deadliest weapons, there were only three of them, not enough to take out the Wither. If only he had an army . . .

He ran back to the cart. He needed to go back, back to that overgrown garden, the vegetable patch. The one with all those pumpkins.

Which lever would send him backward? There were so many rails running out from here down a dozen different tunnels in different directions. If he picked the wrong one, he could end up on the far side of the city.

Stop it. Panicking isn't helping anyone.

Pal climbed onto a pyramid of ore. From up high he saw the layout. The ancients' design. Okay, there was a neat logic to it all. The factory was made of sectors. One was for building materials. Another was for arms and armor; here were rows of anvils waiting. Here was where the enchantment would have taken place. They would have loaded the weapons up and sent them rolling along in carts to be off-loaded and magicked. But then there was the farming sector. He saw the animal pens, the picks and shovels, the row of furnaces that would have been working day and night cooking meat for the castle's vast population. Bowls and buckets still waited upon the long tables, and there were powdery remains of what might have been bushels of wheat. The raw food would have arrived here, been cooked, then been sent out. There was a plan to it all.

Pal settled himself into one of the carts. This was pretty desperate, but this was all he had. "Well? What are you waiting for?"

Good Boy leapt into his lap. Maybe they might end up friends, after all.

Pal reached for the lever beside it. He pulled.

And off he went.

CHAPTER 29

FAITH COLLAPSED AGAINST A wall. Chest burning, legs aching from running, she could barely stand anymore. The breastplate constricted her breathing but she dared not take it off. She just needed to catch her breath. She had to force her fingers to loosen around the sword hilt—but not put it down, no way. She might not have the strength to pick it back up.

Rajah had his head back against the stone wall, his eyes closed as he swallowed great big gulps of air. Even then his hands rested upon his potion bottles, ready to use them the moment danger arose. She hadn't realized quite how much brewing he'd done with Jane back at Mahar Town. Rajah had found his special talent. But would it be enough?

She couldn't hear the Wither. But it was out there, looking for them, stalking the empty halls and corridors, sniffing the air for the scent of the living. Sooner or later it would find them.

"It . . . it seemed to get stronger the more we attacked it," said Rajah. "How is that possible?"

"Nothing about the Wither makes any sense. The thing's got three heads. How does that work?"

Rajah laughed, or at least made a weak rasping sound that could have been a laugh. "If we could only get the three heads to attack one another. Problem solved."

She just nodded.

"Here, Faith. Drink this." Rajah held out one of his potions. "It'll help."

She popped off the cork and swallowed it down. "It tastes horrible."

"One of Jane's special recipes." But moment by moment, the weariness lifted. It was as if she was being filled. A comforting warmth grew in her chest, than spread out along her limbs, right to the tips of her fingertips, making her tingle. She breathed more easily and suddenly the sword, which had seemed almost too heavy to lift, weighed hardly anything. "What was that?"

"A Potion of Regeneration."

"Got any more?" A few more and she could fight all day and take out the Wither once and for all.

He shook his head.

"You didn't keep one for yourself?"

He smiled weakly. "You needed it more than me."

"You've changed a lot, Rajah," said Faith. "Your dad would be proud of you."

"Shame he'll never get to hear about it."

Faith got to her feet. "It's not over yet."

They could run. There was a clear route out. But that was the same route to freedom for the Wither. It had already destroyed this kingdom; what might it do if it was free to roam throughout the surrounding country? What if it got over Lightning Ridge and into the realm itself? No village, no town or city would be safe. The landscape would be one covered with those ominous black roses.

Where were Pal and Good Boy? They'd gotten split up and she knew that was bad. You never split . . . she hoped they were okay. Maybe they were searching for them, Good Boy sniffing out their trail. Maybe they'd gotten away. She wouldn't blame them if they had.

Could she and Rajah destroy it? Just the two of them?

They were low on potions, and she could hit the Wither only so hard. It had floated straight through the lava!

It had been too easy, shooting it from afar with her arrows until it had exploded. She'd thought it was over, the mob boss destroyed, but then it had emerged from the carnage even more powerful, her arrows just glancing off it. So they'd run. The Wither had smashed down the marble walls, never given them a moment's pause, but then they'd found a cart and raced off.

Where were they? Some new, mysterious part of the labyrinth. She had to be careful: Any block could hide a pressure pad, shifting the walls and altering the layout. If you weren't careful you could roam around the castle forever, the path altering behind you.

She froze as she heard its hollow rasp.

"How are you doing?" she asked. Rajah had been badly hit.

He drew his fingers through his beard, singed by the recent explosion. "Ask me later."

They were both sooty from those baleful skulls, but Rajah looked pale. He struggled to stand up straight, his movements slow. Then he caught her worried gaze. "I'm fine. Really."

No point arguing.

"Let's see what we've got." Faith walked to where the floor comprised an intricate pattern made from a variety of plates, ranging from wood to stone, from iron to gold. But was it mere decoration? If she'd learned anything about Castle Redstone, it was that everything in the abandoned city had a hidden purpose.

That sinister rasp was getting louder. It was impossible to work out where it was coming from, but the Wither was getting closer. It wouldn't be long.

One final fight.

Faith readied her bow. "Pick a target."

"A wooden one?"

She nocked an arrow and a moment later it arched through the air, then hit the wooden plate dead-center.

Midway along the corridor two great slabs slammed together.

Rajah nodded. "Nice. Pistons. What about the gold pressure plates?"

Another arrow nocked. The moment it struck the gold plate, flames burst along a section of the corridor.

Faith scowled as she drew another arrow. "Not so great—the Wither's immune to flame. The stone?"

He nodded.

This time . . . nothing. Well, not quite nothing; there was a distant grinding sound, some of the ceiling blocks trembled, dust fell from the cracks between them, but no action. Whatever ancient mechanism the obsidian had once activated was now defunct. Next they tried the iron and again, no reaction.

Rajah gazed along the corridor. "So the iron and stone's safe. If we can get the Wither to chase us along here, we can use the wooden pressure plates against it. Setting them off to crush it. Think it might be enough?"

"We've no guarantee all the plates work. There must be hundreds."

"It's all we've got, Faith."

It just wasn't much. She handed him her bow and quiver. "You'll need these."

"What about you?"

Faith hefted up her sword. "Someone needs to lure it this way."

"We should stick together. You never split the party. That's Rule Number One."

"We've already lost Pal. We need to risk this. It's all or nothing, Rajah." That Wither was definitely close by. Just from which direction? "Don't worry. I'll be coming back this way pretty fast."

"What you mean is I'll only slow you down. I get it. Fine, I'll be waiting. Just don't get lost."

She smiled at him. "See you sooner than you think."

Then she pressed her helmet firmly in place and went searching for the Wither.

CHAPTER 30

PAL PULLED THE CART lever hard the moment he saw the sprawling vegetation. The cart shook, Good Boy yelped as he was thrown forward, and the wheels screeched loudly, but soon the cart rolled to a stop. Good Boy leapt out, and it was a relief to get the big beast off his lap. Then Pal climbed out with the hoe in one hand and a bucket in the other. He needed to work fast. Things had gone quiet within, he hoped because the others had found a chance to escape, or hide, rather than that the Wither had managed to . . .

Don't think about that. They're alive, for now.

Someone, once, had loved this garden. There was a green-house, most of its glass broken now, and there were signs of irrigation channels and low-walled herb gardens. Good Boy ran along the once neatly bordered flower bushes that were now overgrown and merged together. Trees grew in the middle of the fields where the wind had carried their ancient seeds. There was an overabundance of black roses, but he and Good Boy kept clear of them. Good Boy barked.

"What is it? You've found something?"

A pumpkin patch. There were swollen orange bundles sitting on the dirt, vines spreading out in every direction. Pal spat on his hands, took a firm hold of the shovel, and set to work. He needed as many of these as he could gather in a single journey, and even then he didn't know if it would be enough. But the sun was setting and his friends were running out of time. He stabbed the shovel into the dirt and wrenched out the first pumpkin . . .

Where was it? Faith shifted her hold on her sword, her eyes narrowed as she tried to pierce the gloom. Castle Gloom, that was a more fitting name for the place than Redstone. But then who would want to explore a Castle Gloom?

Her footsteps echoed within the empty corridor, her heartbeat almost as loud and yet that was the only sound she could hear. Had the Wither wandered off somewhere? Maybe it had taken a ride in a cart and was now dipping its toes, if it had toes, by the lakeside. Maybe even mobs needed downtime?

Castle Redstone made no sense. Corridors led to blank walls, steps to nowhere, and halls were blocked by collapsed roofs. Light filtered in through the cracks. It was getting dark.

Hunting a Wither through a dark, abandoned ruin. How had she ended up here?

She was scared, but there was more. Excitement.

It had surprised her that as things got worse, she saw things more clearly. She'd felt it when they'd been set upon by those zombies. Even though she'd been elbow-deep in the undead, she'd felt an inner calm, somehow knowing what needed to be done, the steps they needed to take to survive. The others had been too panicked to doubt her. And it had worked.

Perhaps it was just that when you were low on options, what

remained stood out. There was no point moaning about what you couldn't do or how much easier it would be if you could do this instead of that. No, as you ran out of options you just ran faster with the ones you had.

Where was that Wither?

Where was Pal? She'd hoped to find some clue to where he'd disappeared.

One thing at a time. Deal with the—

She stopped.

The creaking was coming from . . . the wall on her left. The mortar between the giant blocks cracked and shook dust across the corridor.

Faith started backing up, but watched the wall shudder.

"Rajah, I hope you've got the arrow ready . . ."

The blocks shook. One shifted a few inches out of place.

She felt the next impact through her feet and into her teeth. The power behind those blows . . .

She tightened her hold on her sword. Suddenly it looked small and feeble. She took another step back.

A little while ago she'd been plain old Faith, new to the realm and tagging along with the son of a famous hero, and his squire. They'd had a few scrapes but nothing serious. She'd expected to be doing those small heroics for a long time. Fighting zombies, taking out skeletons, and making sure they blew up creepers before they got blown up themselves. There were simple tactics to dealing with those levels of mobs. She'd not even been scared the first time the zombies had come shambling out of the darkness. She remembered taking hold of the shovel and smacking the nearest on its head.

Blocks tumbled from the wall and crashed down around her.

A single, hate-filled eye glared through the partial opening. It turned this way and that. Faith stood frozen to her spot. Maybe it wouldn't spot her behind the rubble.

The eye widened.

No such luck.

The next blow brought the entire wall down. Blocks tumbled and crashed all around her, showering her with jagged shards that hissed through the air and ricocheted off her armor, a sliver cutting her cheek.

One massive head emerged from the cloud of dust rolling down the corridor. Then another, and a third. An ominous, dreadful rasp rose up from three throats, and the eyes all filled with deadly hate. The heat intensified as the mob manifested its black wither skulls.

She'd done it. She'd found the horror.

Now it was time to destroy it. Faith glared back at it. "Come on then."

She barely swiped the first wither skull aside with her shield. It exploded against the wall, showering her in burning ash, Faith ducked beneath the second and spun on her heels and started running, the shock wave of the third skull exploding behind her almost knocking her off her feet. Rubble lay scattered throughout the castle. Her heroics would end quickly if she stumbled over a block now.

"I'm coming, Rajah! Be ready!" she shouted. "And I'm bringing a friend!"

This wasn't working. Pal stood there, the pumpkins piled up on the factory floor. They just looked, well, like pumpkins. Good

Boy sniffed at the tunnel entrance, probably trying to pick up Rajah's scent in the chill breeze.

A tremor shook the ground. The tables bounced and iron blocks clanged against one another as that tremor was followed by another, and another. Then what followed was a series of dull and distant explosions.

He took one and put it on the iron assembly. It just sat there, like a pumpkin sitting on a lump of iron. Something was missing.

He stared at the pumpkin. It didn't do anything back.

Was it his imagination or had he just heard someone shout "Rajah"? A someone that sounded a lot like Faith?

Maybe he needed a bigger pumpkin? He swapped it around with one almost twice the size of the first but there was nothing. Maybe it was missing an enchantment? He glanced over at the bookshelves. There was no use in looking there anymore.

More explosions echoed down through the tunnels branching out from the factory. The carts rattled on their tracks, as if eager to get away themselves. He didn't have much time. Faith and Rajah had even less. He needed to get this working right now. But how?

He stared at the pumpkin. It didn't do anything back.

How could it? It was just a pumpkin.

Not a head at all.

Of course. They'd all had proper heads. Heads with *faces*.

Pal grabbed the pumpkin and ran to the nearest table. He swept away the worst of the dust and plonked it down, and then searched through the tools lying upon the adjacent bench. He found a pair of rusty shears; they would have to do. Where should he begin?

Where else? Every head needed a pair of eyes . . .

CHAPTER 31

FAITH SKIDDED AROUND THE corner as the flaming skulls screamed past her and exploded against the opposite wall. The heat wave burned her back, and she coughed as she was wreathed in smoke, but she stumbled on. The floor ahead was checkered and Rajah waved from a distance, his head poking up from behind a pile of rubble.

Stick to the stones. Then you'll be fine.

The Wither swooped toward her, its dry-throated rasp rising to a high-pitched keening. The air around it filled with black particles as the explosive black skulls manifested. Faith slung her shield over her back and charged down the corridor. Smoke, dust, and ash swirled all around her; she could barely see the tiles before her, but she didn't dare slow down. She missed one of the safe stone plates so had to leap to clear of the row of golden traps. An arrow whistled past.

The wall blocks slammed together. The deafening shock wave knocked her off her feet. Faith tumbled over the floor and landed flat on the iron plate.

She needed to catch her breath, just for a moment. The stone plates were safe . . .

An evil hissing sound filled the corridor, and it wasn't coming from the Wither. The hissing increased, and blocks in the ceiling began to open up.

Powder sprinkled down from the opening panels. Faith rubbed the gritty particles between her fingers.

Gunpowder. The iron plate activated TNT hidden along the corridor.

But why hadn't it gone off? She wished Pal was here . . .

Why hadn't it been activated?

She'd landed on the pressure plate hard. Iron was heavy, so maybe it needed additional weight to set it off?

The Wither shrieked as it saw her.

Faith retreated slowly, eyes on the approaching monster, careful to make sure she didn't set off any of the traps herself. "Rajah! Shoot at the iron plate!"

An arrow whistled past her ear and clanged as it struck, the arrowhead neatly piercing the rusty metal.

"Again!"

He shot another. And another. The Wither accelerated.

Another arrow slammed into the iron pressure plate. Was it her imagination or had it moved? The Wither was gaining *fast*.

Every instinct told her to turn and run, but the moment she turned her back she'd be blasted with its exploding skulls.

Another arrow struck the iron pressure plate, joining the thicket of arrows already sticking out of it. How many? Ten?

The plate didn't move.

Then the Wither passed over the iron plate, brushing through the tall stalks of arrows that jutted up like feathered weeds.

The iron pressure plate groaned. That was all the warning Faith got. She spun and yelled. "It's going to blow!"

The sequence wasn't complete, but there was still enough TNT to obliterate the corridor and everything in it. Faith was caught in the shock wave and hurled through the air, spinning uncontrollably, the world blistering white and deafening. Then she crashed against the far wall and was pelted by burning debris. She'd dropped her sword but right now her limbs wouldn't respond. A chunk of stone shattered as it hit the block beside her. A little to the right and she would have been flattened. Through the burning haze she saw Rajah cowering behind his wall. Half of that had been blown away by the explosion, but she saw him moving. Her head rang and her legs were like wet rope; they couldn't straighten.

The echoes of the explosions faded. The dust filling what was left of the corridor settled. The whole area had collapsed in on itself. The walls had been blown away, revealing the redstone circuits and hidden pistons that had activated the traps. But they themselves were in ruin now, the circuit paths broken, the pistons askew, the mechanisms smoking as fiery embers floated in the aftermath.

Rajah hobbled over and held out his hand. "You okay?"

She took it, and had to lean on his to stay upright. "I . . . I think so."

Wow. She was still trembling. Her bones weren't happy with how they'd been treated and needed a little more time to settle back into their right places.

They were both covered in dust. Her armor was badly dented and her shield now just hung off her by its straps, the rest was charcoal, but that was it, that was the worst.

Rajah grinned at her. "We did it."

"We did, didn't we? The iron—"

"—activated the TNT. The pressure panel needed more weight, more objects, to set it off." She gazed at the devastation. "Saved the best till last, eh?"

Her strength was returning and she slowly straightened and stood on her own two feet. Her sword lay a few yards away, wedged in a block. She pressed her boot against the stone and took hold of the hilt with both hands. A huff and pull and the sword was out.

Rajah wiped the dust from his face. "We did it, Faith. We destroyed the terror of Castle Redstone. Now what?"

The Wither was dead. She'd never have believed it possible. It had driven away the entire population of the city, ended a civilization and lurked here for countless centuries, destroying any who had dared explore its vast prison, and now it was gone. "We need to find Pal. He'll be here—"

Blocks rumbled. Small chunks first, tumbling and bouncing off the mounds of broken stone as energy swelled from underneath.

Faith tightened her grip on the sword. Rajah nocked a fresh arrow.

They'd thrown everything they had at it. They'd literally dropped a castle on it, but it still hadn't been enough.

The boulders of rubble burst apart as the Wither exploded out from its tomb, one head after another shaking off the debris until all three were free.

There was nowhere else for them to run to. They'd tried everything and everything had failed.

"I'm sorry I brought you here," said Rajah.

"There's no place I'd rather be," she replied, and it was the truth.

They'd gone into the Nether. They'd crossed the realm, fought guardians, defeated witches, and explored a city no one had set eyes on in centuries. It didn't matter if no one else ever found out what they'd done; she knew, and that was all she'd ever wanted.

The Wither drifted through a haze of swirling black motes. It wasn't rushing now. It knew there was no escape. It wanted to take its time over its triumph.

They wouldn't make it too easy, even if the outcome was inevitable. Heroes went down fighting; it was the only way they knew. Defiant, even in defeat.

Faith tightened her grip on the sword hilt. "Ready?"

The bow creaked as Rajah drew.

Yeah, he was ready.

She couldn't help but grin. They'd made a hero out of him in the end.

CHAPTER 32

PAL STARED AT THE pumpkin. The pumpkin stared back. It wasn't the most accurately carved face and certainly wouldn't win any prizes at the Spring Fair, but it had a pair of lopsided holes for eyes, a sort-of nose, and a smile. Possibly a grimace. But the pumpkin had a face. If this didn't work . . .

He picked up the head and climbed up on the table to reach the empty shoulders of his iron contraption. He lowered the head, muttering prayers to the Creator, and settled it in the center of the shoulders.

And . . . nothing.

Nothing at all.

He'd made a mistake. Those eyes were really lopsided. Maybe he needed to give it another go. He had a dozen or so pumpkins left.

A dozen. A dozen dozen. What difference would it make? He couldn't do it. He'd gotten ahead of himself, needed to remember his place. At the bottom.

A hideous crackling scream echoed from deep down one of the tunnels, followed moments later by a chill gust of wind, of despair. He heard his friends shouting, Faith's battle cry echoing, then withering away to a faint, pitiful whisper.

They needed him. Pal picked up a discarded pickaxe. He wasn't much of a warrior, but there was no other option. At least he'd go down fighting alongside them. At least he'd—

The floor shook at the heavy clang. It was followed by the brutal scraping of iron across stone, then another clang. Good Boy howled and skittered to hide behind a table.

Pal turned and stared at the pumpkin.

The skin turned from its lively orange to gray, from vegetable matter to metal. The head transformed from a lumpy, badly carved pumpkin to a severe, expressionless iron, seamlessly joined to its chunky body.

Now, he'd not expected that. Pal gazed into the empty, lifeless eyes.

Then, starting as flickering embers, the eyes began to glow.

Hit and run. Hit and run. Hit and run.

That was the only strategy they had. But they weren't hitting the Wither hard enough, and they weren't running fast enough. Faith turned around a corner and stopped for breath. She brushed her boots against the wall, her soles smoking from the endless assault of skulls. She was covered in soot. She couldn't keep this up for much longer.

Rajah rested, his head in his hands. His clothes were smoldering rags hanging off his bruised frame. Most of his hair, his crowning feature, had been reduced to crisp stubble. No longer the proud, aloof knight wearing ornately embroidered robes and boots of the softest leather, but a desperate, threadbare survivor. Strangely, the look suited him.

"We need to split up," said Faith. "Force the Wither to go after one or the other. There's nothing to be gained with it hunting us both."

He nodded weakly. "You get going then. I'm just going to rest here for a while longer."

That wasn't what she'd meant. "No, you head off first. I'll distract it a little."

"So it chases you? Why, Faith? If only one of us gets out of here, better that it's you." He raised his head, and there was that old, stuck-up Rajah again. "I order you to save yourself."

She had to laugh. It was hard being all commanding and superior when your eyebrows had been burned off.

Rajah smiled. "You know what the best bit of this adventure was? For me? That day when I cooked the mushroom stew. Us just sitting around the fire, watching it bubble, that smell drifting out of the pot. It reminded me of back home. Being in the kitchen. I always preferred it there. It was warm, cozy, and I loved being wrapped in all the smells and noises. Things bubbling, things crackling, the sound of Cook slamming the dough on the table. I hated the noise of the training field. All those metal things clashing against one another, the horses whinnying—they never sounded happy. They were frightened. Just like me. How about you?"

"Favorite part of this quest? Ask me when we get out of here."

He looked surprised at her answer, or it could have been that without eyebrows he always looked surprised. But he shrugged. "Very well, Faith. I'll ask after."

The shift in the air warned her. A warmer current, and not just the warmth, but also a vague, sickly stench. She hadn't noticed it at first. It was the smell of rot, almost sweet, like the perfume of those black roses that infested the castle. "It's coming."

The shadows swayed and a hellish glow illuminated the dark mouth of the corridor. Then the now familiar rasp, the sound of stale air being pushed through wrinkled, decayed lungs.

Faith stood up. No more hit and run. Rajah joined her. He shook off his weariness and focused his dark gaze upon the approaching Wither. "Maybe it's tired, too?"

It wasn't rushing, that was for sure. It glided along, its three heads almost scraping the ceiling, its eyes pulsing with power. It sensed they were making their last stand, and that suited the Wither just fine.

Rajah frowned and looked around. "Do you hear that?"

The Wither began to quicken.

"Hear what?" Faith wiped the sweat off her palm. It didn't do much good.

"Listen."

To what? All she heard was her breathing, loud and heaving, the crackle of air around the Wither, and . . .

"What is that?" she asked.

It was faint, but it couldn't be missed. A slow, steady pounding coming from elsewhere. There was no way to judge the direction — the walls were too thick and the castle designed to echo with every sound.

"I . . . I thought I heard barking." Rajah shook his head. "But it'll be just our luck if it turned out to be another Wither."

The Wither charged, launching black and blue skulls. They

exploded against the walls, one a few yards before them. Faith batted another aside.

It was a haze. Faith roared as she stabbed, entering the cloak of fear that surrounded the Wither. The netherite sword entered the monster's flesh, or whatever it was made of, and it groaned huskily. Then it swung around, smashing into her and sending her and her sword flying. Faith dimly heard Rajah shouting as he attacked, but her senses were all scrambled by the blow. She lay on the floor, trembling.

But that wasn't her. Something heavy and rhythmic was pounding the ground, sending expanding shock waves through the earth and stone.

Rajah collapsed. He was pale and she couldn't see him breathing. She struggled up. Maybe she could drag him away to somewhere safe. The Wither glided toward her, sensing that she remained a threat.

The walls behind it cracked. Great, thunderous blows struck from the other side, filling the corridor with the sound of iron slamming against stone.

The Wither hesitated, even as it loomed over her, turning its three heads side-to-side, confused.

Blocks fell from the wall and a great cloud of dust swept across, obscuring everything. The Wither hissed angrily.

The wall collapsed to the sound of great thunder. The floor shook so hard the rubble bounced and clattered.

Coughing violently, Faith gazed as figures lurched through the opening in the wall. They were giants, their joints grinding, their heavy feet thudding upon the stone. One after another they marched over the rubble, smashing the fallen stone into dust under their giant iron treads.

And through these metallic giants stumbled a small figure, coughing and waving away the dust with a wolf beside him. Then he looked around until their gazes met.

Pal smiled that wonky half-proud, half-embarrassed smile of his. "Need some help?"

CHAPTER 33

THE IRON GOLEMS MARCHED. *His* iron golems.

Pal had been afraid he was too late. Rajah wasn't moving and Faith looked almost dead. She stared at him, wide-eyed, bewildered.

He'd botched many of the carvings. The features were all over the place. Noses above the eye sockets, mouths running vertically, and in one case an extra eye in the forehead. But slowly each and every one of the thirteen golems had come to life. Starting with an eerie light shining from the eyeholes, then shimmering threads of energy spreading across the vines covering their iron bodies. The air itself had become charged with some strange magic he didn't understand. Then they'd begun to move, to swing their arms on rusty sockets, take faltering steps upon rigid, unbending legs. They'd knocked against one another, swayed dangerously, but eventually gained control of their newly woken bodies. No two were alike, each markedly different from its neighbor not just in the irregular, distorted faces but also in the patterns of rust upon their skin. Some were larger than others, but each was huge. Huge, and unstoppable.

He'd lost his way through the tunnels, unable to work out where the echoes were coming from, until Good Boy had found them. He'd stopped and sniffed at a crack in one of the walls, then jumped and barked excitedly. Pal had ordered his thirteen golems to smash their way through the wall, creating their own shortcut. It didn't matter what the wall was made from, it shattered under the golems' gigantic fists.

They didn't need to be told the Wither was the danger. They surrounded it, swinging their fists, pounding it just as they'd destroyed all the barriers between him and his friends. Pal rushed over to Rajah. Good Boy was already beside him, whimpering. Rajah's skin was cold. "Sire?"

Was he alive?

Good Boy licked Rajah's face, and his eyelids flickered. They opened slowly, gazing at the slobbering face of his wolf. Rajah might have been battered to the breaking point, but he had enough strength to hug his wolf.

Metal shrieked as one of the golems was pulverized by the Wither, its head crunched to pieces. The other golems intensified their attacks, but a few stumbled back, their bodies battered as the Wither fired its skulls directly at them. At this range it couldn't miss. Another golem burst into a thousand molten lumps.

Pal lifted Rajah up, then turned to his other companion. "Faith?"

She looked awful, but relieved. "You . . . you made it. You came back for us."

"The fight's not over," he said. "Those golems can only take so much, and I built them in a hurry."

The Wither slammed another against the floor. It loomed over it, firing a volley of black skulls directly into its chest. The golem cracked, then shattered, hurling iron slivers through the air.

Faith swayed as she got to her feet. "We need to finish this."

"We need to get away. Those golems will keep it busy."

If only he'd had time to build ten more! Even five might have been enough. Another golem collapsed, falling apart as the Wither blasted it.

"Where's my sword?" muttered Faith. She grimaced as she took a step. "Ow."

"Faith . . ."

"Ah. There it is." She limped over and reached under a pile of rubble. A moment later she drew out the netherite sword. "You're a fine craftsman, Pal. I don't think there's a better-made weapon in all the realm."

She wasn't leaving. She was right. They had to finish this.

Pal put Rajah down gently, leaving Good Boy on guard.

Then Pal turned to the battle.

Four golems remained, and each was badly damaged. One was missing an arm and another was half molten slag, but still fighting. The Wither fired a barrage of skulls at one, knocking it back, turning its metallic body red with the heat of its attacks.

"It's trying to escape," said Faith. "What if it gets away? It might have time to regain its strength, then we're back where we started."

The corridor thundered with the sound of the battle. Another golem fell with a ground-shaking thud. Three left and all in battered condition. The Wither, too, had taken an immense beating. Whatever unnatural energies held it together were weakening.

He knew what he needed to do. Pal cupped his hands to his mouth and yelled, "Grab hold of it!"

The golems heard but were slow to respond. The Wither sensed the danger. It screamed and intensified its barrage of skulls. They exploded against a golem, shattering its arm. But it reached out and grabbed the Wither.

The other two did the same, wrapping their arms around the monster, holding it down as it struggled to break free, to fly.

Pal saw the grip slip. The three golems couldn't hold it for another moment. He looked to Faith and—

She ran. She jumped onto a mound of fallen stone and leapt. The Wither and the remaining golems were surrounded by a wall of flame and pools of molten iron but she vaulted through the fire, over the slag, her sword held in both hands.

The Wither twisted one head to face her. The rage rose in its eyes as it summoned another of its skulls. It had Faith in its sights, and its glare froze her heart and filled her soul with despair. She felt the hopelessness eat away at her . . .

Until a golem grabbed its head and twisted it aside. The flaming skulls burst out and flew harmlessly down the corridor.

And Faith struck.

The sword tip entered the Wither dead-center and slid cleanly through its body. Faith had both hands on the hilt and her whole body behind the sword, and the black blade hissed as it was driven hilt-deep.

She'd never forget the sound it made as it died. A scream that came from the darkest place within a heart, a place of pure hate, pure rage and outrage. The sword became chilly, almost too cold to hold, but Faith wanted to make sure, so she only tightened her grip, ignoring the searing pain in her palms. She glared at it with a rage that was purely hers. "Die," she cursed through gritted teeth.

And, its eyes radiating hate till the very last, the Wither did.

Its shadow-wrapped form coalesced as the inverted life-force that had sustained it expired, and its darkness contracted and solidified. Faith collapsed to the floor, the sword limp in her grasp, even as something hard, crystalline, clattered from the evaporating residue of the Wither.

All she heard was her beating heart, the desperate gasps through her raw, constricted throat. She flexed her fingers painfully, allowing the warmth to trickle back into them. She leaned back against the wall and gazed at her three companions.

Good Boy barked, encouraging her on. Rajah? His eyes were bright with pride. He even smiled as he gazed at her. He was burned worse than her, smoke rose from the crispy tuffs of hair he still had, and his beard was crinkled stubble now, but those eyes of his were big and warm and full of celebration.

Pal stood there, his head leaning against the wall, gasping. Then he turned as a clanking echoed out from the dark.

An iron golem shuffled toward them. One leg was mangled, the torso was pitted and blackened with scorch marks, and half its head caved in, smearing its shoulders with molten slag. It stopped before Pal, groaning as it lowered its gaze to him. Pal reached up and put his hand against its cheek. "Nothing I can't fix."

Then Pal looked at Faith and arched an eyebrow. "Are you okay?"

Okay? After all this? Faith smirked.

She was. She really was.

CHAPTER 34

"YOU SURE ABOUT THIS?" Faith asked.

Pal nodded. "I'm staying. There's so much more to be discovered and rebuilt."

"You want to rebuild an entire city?"

They stood in the city square, the epicenter of an ancient civilization that had been the great power of the old kingdoms. Faith squinted, trying to see the city through Pal's eyes, or his imagination. He saw its original grandeur; she saw just rubble.

One of the iron golems lumbered past, arms loaded with stone blocks. It added its armful to the already high pile in the corner. Pal hadn't needed long to rebuild those destroyed by the Wither, and added a few more to his construction workforce. The ruins echoed with the sound of clanking metal feet and the grinding of stone moving against stone.

"It might still be dangerous. We destroyed the Wither but who knows what else might be lurking in the shadows. We should stay, for a while longer."

"These guys will protect me," said Pal, slapping his hand on the back of a passing golem. "And you two need a new adventure now that you've conquered Castle Redstone."

"We've just explored a small corner of it," said Faith. "We'll stay."

"You'll go. The Wither's destroyed, Faith. I'm not like you. I'm a builder, a craftsman. I'm best staying in one place, fixing things nice and slowly. Putting all the broken pieces together. You and Rajah? You want to get over the horizon, feast your eyes upon new lands and mysterious places. But it was a good adventure, I'll admit as much."

"But you're breaking something more important, Pal. What about the three of us? Isn't that worth holding together? Remember Rule Number One? Never separate the party."

Pal paused. She thought she'd won. "Adventuring is your dream, Faith, not mine. We all search for that thing we need to do to be our best selves. You don't see the same beauty I can. How marvelous these redstone circuits could be, what new life they could bring here, once I fix them. What you see as a mishmash of lines and blocks, I see as a beautiful pattern, but it needs to be completed. I can't leave such a puzzle incomplete. I want to see the whole picture, the true extent of its beauty. That's what the original inhabitants were doing here. They didn't separate the function of a thing from it simultaneously being a work of art. That's as much as any craftsman would aspire to. It's broken, Faith, and I can't just leave it like that."

"And have a go at building something bigger and better?"

He grinned. "We understand each other perfectly. No one knows the limits of redstone, if there even are limits. With enough of it, you could light up the whole world. Wouldn't that be something worth striving for? Everything connected? Allowing everyone to share with everyone else."

"A builder, philosopher, and dreamer. You're a strange one indeed, Pal."

Good Boy barked and ran over to her, tail waggling. Rajah appeared moments later, a rucksack over each shoulder. "So you tried to persuade him?"

"I tried," she admitted. "Just not very well, it seems."

Rajah looked from her to his old servant. "I could order you to come."

"But you won't," said Pal. "You don't need me anymore, Rajah. You're your own man. I'm your past now, and the sooner you claim your new life, the better. But you need to leave me here."

"In my past? Then it's over?"

"Yes. This is over. But that's no bad thing. We all got what we wanted, and then some." Pal held out his hand. "But that doesn't mean I won't be sad to see you go, my friend."

"What shall I tell Father?" asked Rajah.

"Tales of your great adventure, what else?"

"*Our* great adventure," said Rajah. "When the bards sing the tale, I'll make sure they put you in the title."

"How about that? Glory, too." Pal pulled out the star stone he'd taken from the remains of the Wither. "If anything happens, if I need you, I'll send a signal. It won't matter how far you are, you'll see it."

Faith hugged him. She didn't want to let go, didn't want this last moment that it was the three of them to end. Pal hugged her back and whispered. "Look after him."

She nodded as they separated. Then she slung her own rucksack over her shoulders. She tightened her sword belt one notch, feeling the reassuring weight of the netherite sword on her left hip. She was suddenly aware of the flagstones under her feet. There was a current flowing, wanting to carry her along to some new place. The compulsion, the desire, to get moving was irresistible, and as powerful as Pal's desire to stay. They had different destinies. The sooner they got started, the better.

The wind picked up. It carried whispers, promises even. *Come! Follow! See what's next! There's always a new horizon.*

Rajah whistled and Good Boy sprang to his side. The wolf peered at Pal. They'd never been friends. The wolf had a wandering soul, too. He slapped his tail on the ground, eager to be off.

Rajah nodded at his oldest friend. There weren't words adequate to say how they felt about going their separate ways. Faith wiped her eyes and gave Pal a wan smile. Then she started walking, Rajah beside her, Good Boy sprinting ahead, sniffing the way through the old city. He barked, beckoning along, wanting them to hurry.

She did look back, of course she did. On the crest of a hill, with the wilderness ahead and the vastness of Castle Redstone behind. One last look.

Pal sat upon a wall, chin on his fist, gazing at a disjointed redstone circuit upon the ground. The lines ran up the walls and across the roofs like jungle vine. She couldn't make any sense of it; it was like trying to untangle a pile of wool after a kitten had finished playing with it. Where did it start?

Then Pal jumped down from his perch and from the bag on his belt began pouring out the redstone dust, creating new connections and repairing old ones. Around him the iron golems continued their work. They would not stop, no need to rest. Maybe his ambition to rebuild an entire city wasn't as wild or foolish as it sounded. Pal completed his fixes, brushed the remaining dust off his hands, then stood upon a pad.

Blocks slid apart. Water trickled down along gullies. The fountains began to fill. The stream spread outward toward the dusty irrigation channels and fallow fields.

Rajah clapped. "He's quite a clever fellow, don't you think?"

"We could do with him coming along." She still couldn't let go of the idea.

Pal, in the distance, heard the clap. Faith's heart quickened. He'd changed his mind. But, instead, Pal pulled off his cap and waved it at them.

She waved back. It was goodbye.

And that was the last she saw of him.

THEY'D PICKED A PLACE that, if it wasn't quite wild, was certainly beyond the signs of civilization. There were mountains to their back, and a few scattered villages where they traded every now and then. And despite all this time, Faith still couldn't fathom the local language.

Good Boy slept by the fire. His fur was more white now than gray—"Old Boy" suited him better nowadays—but his bark as lively as ever. His ears twitched and he scrabbled, lost in some dream of chasing, in some dream of adventure.

Faith still dreamed of adventure. She would have thought after her lifetime full of it there'd be no room left. That was the business of younger folk than her. *Much* younger.

They passed by en route to whatever quest was fresh; sometimes they'd stop for a meal, for a bed. For a story. They'd enter the house, kick off the mud, their faces fresh with the harsh wind and the thrill of what lay ahead, full of chatter of the beasts they'd conquer and the treasures they'd claim, then, slowly but inevitably, they'd fall quiet, as they saw. Faith liked it a little dim. She said it was easier to ignore the dust, but truth was her old eyes just preferred the twilight now. And if she was being honest, the dimness brought your attention to where it mattered. The trophies of her life. Her story.

Was that really the skull of an Ender Dragon? Did those elytra still work? Whose armor was that, the set made of pure netherite? And the still, who brewed all these potions? They'd gasp at the iron golem, all rusty now, standing in the corner.

They'd stare at the trophies, then turn back to her, unable to marry the old woman before them with vast treasure trove. Then Rajah would come out of the kitchen with some fresh bread and a plate of chops and they'd gather, eat, and tell tales.

Rajah, yeah, that was a thing. She'd thought, after Castle Redstone, they'd go their separate ways. But somehow they didn't. There was more to tell about that relationship, but that wasn't for sharing with strangers. But no one much mentioned Lord Maharajah nowadays.

Did she still crave it? Of course. Each time their visitors would pack and leave she would watch from the door, envious. But then the old envy the young, no two ways about it. Then she felt the ache in her shoulders, the stiffness in her knees, and laughed at herself, foolish old woman, then settled back beside the fire to give Good Boy a good ruffle. She had nothing left to prove. But still, who didn't dream about that one last, grand adventure? Good Boy barked in his dream. There you go, Good Boy certainly did.

What was he cooking? Whatever it was, it smelled delicious. "Hurry up, will you? I'm starving!"

"It'll be ready when it's ready!"

Pie? It had been a while since they'd had pumpkin pie. One of Rajah's specialties.

She should go do her rounds. The animals were all in their shelters for the night, but you never knew what else might be out there. True, most hostile mobs knew enough to avoid them, but zombies had no brains, and it was only last month a creeper had blown up half the shed.

Good Boy stirred. The smells must have gotten to him, too. He shook himself awake and looked around as he stood. Foolish old dog. Didn't he know where he was? Then Good Boy barked.

"Hush now, you'll have your dinner the same time as the rest of us."

He barked again, then dashed out the door.

"Good Boy! Get back in here!"

"There. Get the plates out." Rajah appeared at the door with a steaming, freshly baked pie on a tray. Then he heard Good Boy. "What's up with him?"

"How would I know? He's your dog."

"Go look. I'm holding the pie."

Faith sighed as she rose from her chair. Just when she'd gotten warm and comfortable. That dog was sleeping outside tonight, no two ways about it.

Good Boy was jumping and barking as if he'd found a cat up a tree.

"Calm down! You'll put your hip out if you carry on like that! You're not a puppy anymore!"

He wasn't listening. The sheep began stirring. Great. Good Boy had set them off. They'd be up now, all night, bleating. No sleep for her. Faith joined the frantic beast. "Will you just calm down. You're too old for this . . ."

Oh. Now, that was a thing.

"Rajah. You need to come out and see this."

"But the pie's getting cold!"

It was going to get a lot colder before they'd get around to eating it. "Just come and look."

"This had better be worth it. That pie . . . oh. I see. Well, that's a thing for sure. Pal?"

"Who else?"

Rajah chewed the tip of his mustache. "All these years and nothing. Not a word. I guess I'd better pack the pie for the journey."

"And you'll need to brew up some fresh potions. Double strength."

"Do I tell you your business? No, I don't. I'll need to pack the ointment for your knees."

"My knees are fine," she grumbled, ignoring the ache from having gotten up out of the seat too fast.

The sky beam blazed from beyond the horizon. It shimmered against the velvet blackness of the night sky, casting its glow upon the mountaintops. He'd said he'd send a signal.

Typical Pal. Always showing off.

She left Good Boy barking. Faith stood in the hall, hands on hips. There was the sound of shattering glass from the laboratory, and Rajah swore. He was getting clumsy in his old age.

Faith strode across the room to the mantelpiece, the ache suddenly gone. It hung over the mantelpiece, gathering dust like everything else in this house, including her. Time to wipe it off and see if there was still some life in it. Faith grasped the hilt of her netherite sword, and the moment her fingers tightened she felt filled with strength. Just like the old times. She lifted it off the hook and drew it from the scabbard. The firelight shone upon its perfectly sharp edge; the black metal shone like oil on water, alive with power, with excitement. Just like her.

It was time for a new adventure.

ABOUT THE AUTHOR

SARWAT CHADDA spent twenty years as an engineer before turning his hand to writing. Since then he's written novels, comic books, and TV series, including *Devil's Kiss*, *City of the Plague God*, and *Baahubali: The Lost Legends*. His writing embraces his heritage, combining East and West, with a particular passion for epic legends, vicious monsters, glorious heroes, and despicable villains. Having spent years traveling the Far East, he now lives in London with his family, but has a rucksack and notebook on standby.

Twitter: @sarwatchadda
Instagram: @sarwat_chadda

ABOUT THE TYPE

This book was set in Electra, a typeface designed for Linotype by W. A. Dwiggins, the renowned type designer (1880–1956). Electra is a fluid typeface, avoiding the contrasts of thick and thin strokes that are prevalent in most modern typefaces.

DISCOVER MORE MINECRAFT
HAVE YOU READ THEM ALL?

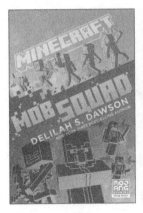

- [ ] *The Island* by Max Brooks
- [ ] *The Crash* by Tracey Baptiste
- [ ] *The Lost Journals* by Mur Lafferty
- [ ] *The End* by Catherynne M. Valente
- [ ] *The Voyage* by Jason Fry
- [ ] *The Rise of the Arch-Illager* by Matt Forbeck
- [ ] *The Shipwreck* by C. B. Lee
- [ ] *The Mountain* by Max Brooks
- [ ] *The Dragon* by Nicky Drayden
- [ ] *Mob Squad* by Delilah S. Dawson
- [ ] *The Haven Trials* by Suyi Davies
- [ ] *Mob Squad: Never Say Nether* by Delilah S. Dawson
- [ ] *Zombies!* by Nick Eliopulos
- [ ] *Mob Squad: Don't Fear the Creeper* by Delilah S. Dawson
- [ ] *Castle Redstone* by Sarwat Chadda

Penguin
Random
House

DISCOVER MORE MINECRAFT

LEVEL UP YOUR GAME WITH THE OFFICIAL GUIDES

- ☐ *Guide to Combat*
- ☐ *Guide to Creative*
- ☐ *Guide to Enchantments & Potions*
- ☐ *Guide to Farming*
- ☐ *Guide to Minecraft Dungeons*
- ☐ *Guide to Ocean Survival*
- ☐ *Guide to the Nether & the End*
- ☐ *Guide to PVP Minigames*
- ☐ *Guide to Redstone*
- ☐ *Guide to Survival*

MORE MINECRAFT:

- ☐ *Amazing Bite-Size Builds*
- ☐ *Bite-Size Builds*
- ☐ *Blockopedia*
- ☐ *Epic Bases*
- ☐ *Epic Inventions*
- ☐ *Exploded Builds: Medieval Fortress*
- ☐ *Let's Build! Land of Zombies*
- ☐ *Let's Build! Theme Park Adventure*
- ☐ *Maps*
- ☐ *Master Builds*
- ☐ *Minecraft for Beginners*
- ☐ *Mobestiary*
- ☐ *The Survivors' Book of Secrets*

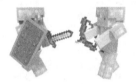

Penguin
Random
House